LOVE STORIES ACROSS TIME AND HISTORY

LOVE STORIES ACROSS TIME AND HISTORY

Compiled by
Abhishek Rana

Vitasta

Dedicated
to all the lovers

Published by
Renu Kaul Verma
Vitasta Publishing Pvt Ltd
4348/4C, Ansari Road, Daryaganj
New Delhi - 110 002
info@vitastapublishing.com

ISBN: 978-81-19670-87-1

First Edition 2024
MRP ₹350

Edited by Shailaja Nair
Typeset & Cover Design by Somesh Kumar Mishra
Printed by Vikas Computer and Printers, New Delhi

Contents

Publisher's Note

The best kind of love stories are the ones that completely immerse readers in the emotions of its characters. They reveal the beauty behind the pain, the lust within the passion and honour hand in hand with the sacrifice experienced by the lovers. All in all, immortal love stories are majestic because of their very humanness. They occupy an ocean of feelings just between two principal characters.

These diverse tales are populated with characters who have to make difficult choices and choose to carve their own paths even when people around them oppose their decisions. Their love clashes with society and their own sense of identity. Their actions are just as political as they are personal. The timelessness of these stories resides in the fact that they're all rooted in frank human behavior that can be identified with. Orpheus's grief for Eurydice is just as palpable to the reader as Liang Shanbo's struggle to break out of her familial bonds that restrain her from living her life to its fullest. Amrita Pritam's yearning for Sahir Ludhianvi is as conflicted as Inessa Armand's attraction to Vladimir Lenin.

The way we perceive love stories is skewed by our desire for them to be perfect and often happy. The most memorable love stories around the world end in tragedies. This is because the reality of love is often harsher than the fantasy we create in our minds. However, there is no scarcity of tenderness, humour and romance here either. These stories span centuries continents and race; they've been taken from myths, folktales and history to give a more rounded representation.

Every country and place on earth has a love story that speaks to people with its themes of valour, transgression, and duty. This collection hopes to bring these stories to a wider readership so that they can also experience all the possible shades of love that transcend man-made boundaries to reach your heart.

The Butterfly Lovers

Zhu Yingtai was standing in line, awaiting her turn to be inspected by the teachers at the academy. Behind her, Liang Shanbo was trying not to fall asleep.

'How long are they going to take?' He whispered to her. 'Shouldn't they be doing this after the students have had some sleep?'

Zhu Yingtai bristled. She had been dreading the inspection ever since she had left Shangyu. Her disguise had fooled everyone till now, including her new friend, but she was afraid that the scholars at the academy might discover the truth and send her back home. Or they could call the higher authorities and have her arrested for cheating them.

This story comes from China.

All she'd wanted was to come to the capital and study at the academy under the scholarly supervision of the teachers. It had taken a lot of effort and constant pleading to convince her father that she could don a convincing disguise that'd be able to fool people into believing that she was a man.

'Next!' The peon called out from the end of the room. Zhu Yingtai stepped forward and went to the tiny room where she found a bald little official, nearly blind, sitting cross-legged on a marble plinth. He looked at her with his rheumy eyes and remarked: 'They're making them a little too soft these days.'

Zhu Yingtai stood straight, trying not to betray any feminine characteristics. She had trained herself by copying her father's mannerisms and knew that no man ever loosened himself in the presence of an elder. It was important to show respect by standing still and letting them inspect you without showing any sign of rebellion.

The old man peered at the boy standing before him. He was certainly disciplined but could turn out to be one of those annoying eager-to-please oafs who thought they could get further in their career just by dint of flattery.

'Come closer,' he ordered the boy, who acquiesced.

Zhu Yingtai shivered under the layers of clothes she was wearing to hide her true self. The old man had a sharp gaze despite the wrinkles around his eyes and would find her out immediately if he looked closely.

The old man shifted in his seat. There was something wrong with this boy. He was standing a little too erect and beneath his placid expression, the old man could sense a storm of worry brewing.

'What is it, boy?' the old man asked, making the boy jump in surprise.

'I'm just…just nervous, sir,' Zhu Yingtai said. Her voice sounded too shrill to herself, even more so than her original tone.

The old man silently appraised the boy before him. He certainly looked meek, and his voice, which hadn't broken yet, seemed to put him in the category of those shy, impressionable ones who always had their noses buried in their books and didn't know half of what was going on around them. That could be a problem, but he was certain that the academy would weed out any remaining innocence from his body during his stay here.

'Don't forget that you're here to honour your family,' he said sternly. 'The Academy is home to sacred knowledge and its students are mere vessels that must contain whatever amount fits into them. Nothing less, nothing more. Do not think of transgressing from your role or else you will only bring shame to your loved ones. Leave now and prepare to work hard.'

Zhu Yingtai nodded vigorously and left the room in a hurry before the old man could detect anything more about her.

She met Liang Shanbo on her way to classes the next day. He was standing in the corridor with his books, as if he'd been waiting for her.

'Oh, hi,' Zhu Yingtai said with a frown. 'Don't you

want to get inside before the master arrives?'

'Hi, I was waiting for you,' Liang Shanbo said cheerfully. 'How was your meeting with the old master?'

'Well, it was fine. I'm still here, aren't I?' she said, trying to side-step him and enter the room.

'I knew you'd do well,' Liang Shanbo said. 'I didn't even know what he'd ask. I was so afraid that he'd expel me after he said that my face had mischievous features, but then he changed his mind and let me go.'

'He seemed a little bit batty,' Zhu Yingtai confessed. 'Didn't seem like he was all there in his mind.'

'Hmm, could be,' Liang Shanbo said. 'But, in that case, the school shouldn't get him to evaluate the students. Who knows how many bad decisions he might make.'

Zhu Yingtai nodded. 'You're right,' she said. 'But let's go inside and wait for the master. We can talk after the lesson.'

'Oh, yes, yes,' Liang Shanbo said, and stepped aside to let her pass.

They spent the whole period, and the rest of the day seated next to each other and became inseparable from that day onward.

Zhu Yingtai didn't know what it was about Liang Shanbo that attracted her to him. Perhaps it was the fact that he didn't take things as seriously as everyone else at the Academy. He was a diligent worker, but never worried about proving himself to anybody. He carried himself with ease and respected everyone. With Zhu Yingtai he was even more casual, which made her feel free as well. Maybe that was what she liked about him. Zhu Yingtai realised that he was the only one who made her feel like she could express herself in a way that she had never thought was possible before.

So, they would talk late into night, sitting beside each other. Liang Shanbo told her about his childhood and how much fun he used to have during the summer.

'We used to run down the streets barefoot till our feet were blistered and raw,' he told her, his cheeks flushed with the heady rush of memory. 'But we didn't care at all. We didn't care about our neighbours either. Aunt Daiyu was always in an unpleasant mood when we were screaming and playing in the streets. She used to bang her utensils to make her displeasure known.'

Zhu Yingtai was impressed and a little jealous. While Liang Shanbo had spent his childhood in blissful freedom, she had been brought up in a household that wanted nothing from its children but piety and discipline.

'It was very different at our home,' she said, after Liang Shanbo prodded her to recount her childhood. 'We didn't have as much fun as you did. My father is a very strict man. He loves rules and discipline. He doesn't have much use for fun.'

Liang Shanbo smiled. 'No wonder you're always so serious,' he said.

'No, I'm not,' Zhu Yingtai protested. 'Maybe I haven't met a person with whom I can have fun with, yet,' she added with a smirk.

'Oh, come on,' Liang Shanbo said, smiling even more

widely. 'You know that's a lie because I saw how happy you were when you played with those celebratory flags I gave you last week. You were just like a child.'

'I didn't realise you were watching me play!' Zhu Yingtai cried, and then suddenly stopped.

She'd almost forgotten that she was in disguise. Her voice had broken the coarse pitch and she sounded like a hot steaming whistle.

'I just got excited,' she said, coughing to hide her mistake. 'I had a throat infection when I was a child and it affected my voice. It didn't develop with age.'

Liang Shanbo waved it off. 'It's alright,' he said. 'Even my voice does that sometimes when I'm in front of Master Donghai.'

Zhu Yingtai laughed, relieved that Liang Shanbo didn't suspect anything. They continued to talk about other, less consequential things. It was then that Zhu Yingtai first felt the first stirrings of love.

Zhu Yingtai found herself thinking about Liang Shanbo every moment when she wasn't occupied with work. But she didn't think about him as a friend. Her daydreams had got woozier. She thought about his long lashes, his lips that formed a perfect bow, and how his eyes crinkled when he smiled. She spent a lot of time imagining talking with him about things unrelated to studies. She liked his company, and cracked jokes with him like she wouldn't dare back home. It was liberating to be a man because everything seemed possible and within her reach. But could she love someone while hiding the essential truth about herself from him?

Was this even love? Zhu Yingtai had always known that her heart wasn't her own to give to any man. Like any woman in China, her union would be decided by her parents. Her duties as a wife had been ordained, and all she could do was follow them without rebelling and she'd have a good and long life.

Love, her mother had warned, was for weak people who didn't know how to adhere to the rules laid out by the divine powers. Zhu Yingtai had never argued with her mother's restricted ideas of romantic love because to her, the emotion was a phenomenon that made people do terrible things to others and themselves.

And yet, despite knowing that her mother was right, and that love led to ruin, she couldn't separate herself from what she felt for Liang Shanbo.

They were going to meet in the evening again. Zhu Yingtai had decided to tell the truth to Liang Shanbo. She'd explain why she had to wear a disguise to study, and how she'd found herself attracted to him despite trying to keep a distance between them. Falling in love wasn't a mistake or a sin, Zhu Yingtai felt, but deceiving someone was.

If Liang Shanbo rejected her, she'd leave the Academy and go back home.

They met under the pavilion of the city bridge. It was evening. The sky had turned a golden orange with the glow of the setting sun. Liang Shanbo had hurt his hand while carrying water.

Zhu Yingtai held his hand and caressed it.

'Your skin is too soft!' Liang Shanbo exclaimed. 'Have you never done any work in your life? Always pampered, eh?'

'No, it's not like that,' Zhu Yingtai said quickly. 'I… I used to be a very sick child, so my parents thought it better to not put me through physical labour.'

'Oh, and you're fine now?' Liang Shanbo asked. He was genuinely concerned about her. She could see it in his eyes; the way they softened when he looked at her.

'Yes, yes I am,' she said. 'As fine as I can be.'

'I… I am not what you think I am,' she said.

'What do you mean?' Liang Shanbo asked her, perplexed at her serious tone.

'I'm not a man,' Zhu Yingtai said. 'I'm a woman and I have been under disguise these past few years because I wanted to study at the Academy and it was the only way I could successfully gain an education that is otherwise only meant for men in this kingdom.'

This new information had a peculiar effect on Liang Shanbo. He didn't look enraged or betrayed, but there was a little bit of disappointment in his eyes.

'Why didn't you tell me all this before?' he asked her. 'Did you have doubts that I'd reveal your identity to the Academy pupils? You didn't trust me enough?'

'It wasn't like that,' she said. 'I didn't know what I felt toward you for the longest time. I kept trying to understand what I felt for you. I didn't want to ruin our friendship by telling you the truth. I loved spending time with you. I was never as free with a human being as when I was with you.'

The spark in Liang Shanbo's eyes came alive again.

'Do you mean to say that you have a fondness for me?' he asked.

Zhu Yingtai didn't hesitate to say yes. And they embraced each other.

It was the happiest she had ever felt. She had never expected Liang Shanbo to accept her, and now that he had, she didn't want to be away from him. They both made plans to travel back to their homes and tell their parents the truth. Once they had been informed, the two families could meet and decide the right time for marriage.

They parted ways at the same spot where they had met for the first time. As Zhu Yingtai watched Liang Shanbo's figure recede in the distance, she felt a sharp pain in her side, as if something had been wrenched from her body. She didn't pay much attention to it. Only when she reached home did she realise that the fates had been trying to warn her of the darkness ahead.

Her father listened to her love story, and promptly denied his permission to her marrying Liang Shanbo. He told her that he'd already decided a match for her.

'You can't decide my fate like this, father,' she cried. 'I have sworn myself to someone else.'

'Does he know that you attended the university in disguise?' her father asked.

'And what if he does know about it?' she asked

angrily. 'Are you ashamed that your daughter has become a scholar?'

'You don't know anything,' her father said. 'You're young and foolish. You may not care about what others speak about you, but our family's honour depends on how society perceives us, and I can't let you tarnish our image like this. Who is the boy?'

'He was my classmate at the Academy,' she said. 'I revealed the truth about myself to him before coming to home. He knows me and he loves me. Please accept this union, father.'

'No,' her father thundered. 'That is not an option. You must forget the boy or else...'

'Or else what? What are you going to do?' she asked, suddenly unafraid of any punishment. 'Kill me because I dared to love someone? I'll make your task easier by taking myself out.'

Her father laughed.

'As I said, you're young and foolish,' he said with a glacial smile. 'I will not kill you or forsake you, because you have been promised to Ma Wencai, who's a wealthy merchant and does a lot of travelling. You'll be happy with him, and in time, you'll forget that boy as well. The ardour of youth seldom lasts more than a few months.'

Zhu Yingtai didn't know if her father was telling the truth. She had, after all, not lived long enough to know about the mysteries of love, and it was true that Liang Shanbo was one of the first men in the outside world with whom she had interacted. But that didn't change how she felt about him. Liang Shanbo could've met her at any stage of her life, and she'd still love him as much as she did now. Her father knew about love between physical beings, but he had no knowledge of the love between souls that had been joined in heaven with the blessings of the divine powers. And if mortals had decided that their union on earth was impossible, she would meet her beloved in death, she decided.

She lunged at the table, fell to her knees, and grabbed the knife from the fruit bowl. Then she stood up hurriedly and whirled around to face her father with the knife scraping her throat.

'If I must die, it shall be for love. I will not let my soul perish by marrying another man.'

For a moment, her father was afraid of what she might do. He imagined her limp body falling to the floor with a thud, the spurt of blood staining the wooden planks. He had always believed that Zhu Yingtai was the most mature among his children, but now she was about to take her life because of some unworthy man.

Her hand was trembling. She clearly hadn't planned on harming herself, which meant she wouldn't do it.

'Won't you even think about the agony your mother will face once you're gone?' he said softly, and inched closer to her.

'If she can't accept my love for him, who has been bound to me for life, then perhaps she is responsible for both of our pain,' Zhu Yingtai said. She drew the blade closer and winced as the blade nicked her skin.

She had been so agile and quick in her childhood, her father thought. He had seen her play ball in the garden and climb trees like a squirrel. And now, just as quickly, she'd be dead.

With a viper like snap of his arm, he wrenched the knife out of her hand, and threw it out the window. And before she could rush out or harm herself further, her father raised his hand and struck her across the face so hard that the poor girl fell into his arms, unconscious.

Zhu Yingtai was married to Ma Wencai in a quiet ceremony. She was sedated with poppy seeds and dressed in the plainest of clothes. Ma Wencai, who was old enough to be her father, didn't care about her beauty and intellect. He'd only married her to enhance his status in society. She'd fulfil her wifely duties, and he'd fulfil his desires. That was the extent of their relationship.

When it was time to go, Zhu Yingtai refused to look into her father's face. She embraced her mother, and whispered to her that they were the reason for their daughter's ruin.

On the way to Ma Wencai's abode, stormy winds lashed at the procession, tearing into the flags, and snagging the curtains of the palanquin so much that it was difficult to advance. They decided to wait till the storm had passed on.

There were murmurs among the palanquin bearers that the weather turning was a bad omen and that the bride would bring bad luck to her lord's house.

Zhu Yingtai didn't hear their whispers. She sat silently

and stared at her hands. She felt detached from her body. In her mind, she was still with Liang Shanbo. They didn't need the physical plane of existence to justify their love story.

Suddenly, she felt a tug beneath her ribs. She parted the curtains and looked out. They had stopped before a graveyard. Zhu Yingtai squinted, trying to discern the faded lettering on the tombstones.

'I'm stepping out,' she told palanquin bearers, and jumped out into the cold.

Zhu Yingtai narrowed her eyes and looked into the distance. There stood a tombstone that was in a better condition than the others. Its marble was still smooth, and the name on the stone was legible.

She looked again, and this time, she read the name written on the grave.

It was as if the gods themselves had brought her to this place to finally meet her loved one. At the sight of Liang Shanbo's resting place, Zhu Yingtai fell to her knees. The divine powers had made this possible. If they couldn't be together in life, then their union must be written in death.

Zhu Yingtai got up hastily, gathering her dress above her ankles, and ran toward Liang Shanbo's grave.

'I never expected to be away from you,' she sobbed, falling to her knees before the tombstone. 'I should never have hidden my truth from you. If I had told you about myself before, we could've run away and stayed together forever. Now all my words are useless.'

Oh, if only she could be with him!

The agony of being separated from Liang Shanbo was something she didn't want to suffer anymore.

'Let me in, let me in, Liang Shanbo,' she screamed and started beating her hands on the tombstone.

She kept at it until they were raw and bloody. She didn't care anymore.

Suddenly, she heard a crack and a loud snap as the stone broke in half. Zhu Yingtai looked at her beloved's face down below and swore that she hadn't seen anything more beautiful. She drew a deep breath and walked down into the grave to join him where he lay in peace.

The winds calmed down after Zhu Yingtai joined Liang Shanbo in death. The palanquin bearers tried to find their mistress, but they couldn't find anything that belonged to her. The only thing in the graveyard that caught their attention were two butterflies that seemed to have flown out of a nondescript grave, toward the heavens, keeping close to each other, so they'd never be separated again.

Dante and Beatrice

Dante's hands trembled as he read the scroll. The words had lost their meaning. They appeared on the parchment like the scribbling of an indisposed man sunk into a delirium. It couldn't be true. She was so young.

'What is it?' Gemma asked him. 'Is it bad?'

Dante turned away from her and walked to the window. He parted the curtains and looked out. The day was fresh and bright. The sky was clear. The birds chirped merrily in the trees and the benign sunlight fell on the plants in the garden that emphasised their beauty. That wasn't how it was supposed to be. Why didn't the sky tear itself into shreds, and the earth open its parched mouth to gorge on every living thing? Why had beauty persisted in the world when it was bereft of life, leaving

---

This story comes from Italy.

everything in a state of dreamlike sheen that was only an approximation of life?

Dante looked into the dusty gloom of the drawing-room. His wife's face seemed to float out of the darkness toward him. She was concerned about him. Gemma stretched out her hand wordlessly toward him. Dante clutched the letter tighter in his fist and stepped away from the window.

'She is dead,' he said, not looking at Gemma. He couldn't speak her name or face his wife to tell her what had happened. He could sense the early signs of convulsive grief and wanted to be alone before it could drag him down into the depths of helpless despair.

'Who is dead?' Gemma asked. Her arm was still stretched out, hoping to take the parchment away from him. She'd seen him read the letter in a frenzied state, every word bringing about an explosion of feelings that he could barely keep within himself. She knew he wouldn't be willing to tell her the truth, but she had to try.

'Someone I used to know,' Dante said. He was staring at the now wrinkled parchment in his palm.

'Who?' Gemma asked again. She was insistent, nagging, but there was no other way to engage with her husband. They'd lived their brief married life in a clinical togetherness and she knew that this detachment could soon turn into a hard wall of silent resentment that would be impossible to crack open.

'Someone,' Dante said. The finality in his voice made Gemma bristle. So, he didn't want to tell her about the woman. Good. She would leave him alone to rot in his grief.

'I will leave you to it then,' she said, barely hiding the contempt in her voice.

'No, stay,' Dante said, his voice almost cracking with his grief. 'I'm going to the study. I have work to do.'

Gemma watched as he rushed out of the room. He looked stricken. Sick. Gemma sat back on her stool and took up her needlework. She knew he wouldn't be coming out of the study any time soon.

***

Dante adjusted the wick and set the lamp on the table. His study was spare, with a table below the window to let the sunlight seep in while he worked in the mornings. He sat back in his chair and bowed his head. He felt too numb to cry. There were too many thoughts swirling around in his head that it was impossible to pick one from the tangle and introspect.

He'd met Beatrice only twice. The first time he'd seen her, they'd been children. He hadn't known what love meant then, but something had happened to him when he'd looked at her. The most maudlin explanation of romantic obsession is that it emerges through the appreciation of the beauty and uniqueness of the object of desire. However, the spell of love only sustains itself and even strengthens with time if the beholder recognises the invisible thread of connection that binds two souls together. As a child, Dante had felt something similar when he had first met Beatrice.

Presently, Dante closed his eyes and let the memories of their first meeting wash over him.

They were both nine years old. He was a few months older than her but looked young for his age.

Dante had come to the May Day party. The Portinari house was grand and lavish. It was surrounded by green fields and a copse of trees. The path to the main building was strewn with pebbles, and Dante had already filled his pockets with them as he tottered to the entrance, hand in hand with his father.

'Remember, you must behave yourself, my son,' Alighiero di Bellincione told his son. 'The Portinari family is very well respected, so we must maintain the decorum of their house.

'Yes, father,' Dante said, running through the gates.

The Portinari family had spared no expense for the party. The grounds were interspersed with tables bearing all kinds of food and beverages. Women and girls danced around the maypole, their white robes fluttering in the wind.

Dante was looking around for his friends when he saw something that surprised him. A girl about his age with a rose behind her ears, and another one in her hand, was walking serenely, ripping the petals and throwing them on the ground. The way her fingers were ripping the petals, Dante assumed the girl was very angry. But her overall calm demeanour seemed to indicate otherwise. He approached her.

'What are you doing?' he asked, as he drew near to her.

The girl turned to look at him and frowned.

'None of your business,' she said.

Dante felt something strange in his stomach when he looked at the girl. It wasn't the lustrous red hair or her big bright eyes. It wasn't how the light fell on her face as she turned, adding to her luminescence. It wasn't the downward turn of her mouth or the mole on her neck. All these little things made her look distinctive from everyone else at the party, but what struck Dante was the firmness and control in her voice. Immediately, Dante felt like he recognised that voice, or the tone of it, even though he had no idea how it could be possible because he had never met Beatrice before and didn't know anybody who sounded like her. The familiarity was further accentuated by how she was looking at him. Her gaze was surprisingly direct and had the effect of almost boring into a person's soul. Dante stumbled.

'Sorry, I didn't mean to be offensive,' he said.

Beatrice nodded slowly.

'Okay,' she said and left him standing alone amidst the revelry of the first day of summer.

That was it. Their first meeting had been abrupt and inconsequential. It didn't have the trappings of any emotion unless Beatrice's momentary annoyance could be construed as a feeling that would stay with them for a long time.

Despite the brevity of their meeting, Dante was unable to forget Beatrice. It was almost comical how she began to encroach on his thoughts after that day. He would be walking down the stairs or eating breakfast, and suddenly, he'd be thinking of the scene at the Portinari grounds. He kept coming back to it, against his wish. There was no escape from it, and neither was there any meaning to the interaction that he could decipher. What was the point of the memory still replaying in his head?

How could you fall in love with someone you barely knew? It seemed stupid. Love was based on familiarity. It couldn't grow just by itself without the anchor of a relationship. Dante knew all this and yet his mind didn't agree. There must be some feelings that were beyond definition. Love as people knew it was only concerned with the body of a person. It hardly ever reached far enough to touch the soul. Perhaps, the reason people laughed at the idea of such love was that they were incapable of experiencing it. Dante's feelings for Beatrice were entirely sacred. He didn't want to have his way with her. He just wanted to hold on to the shimmering motes that disappeared when she moved. He wanted to follow her steps and touch the soft earth that bore the imprint of her feet. He wanted to write down all the words she had spoken to him so that he could make a song from them. He wanted to sew all the moments he had shared with her into the fabric of his being so he would never have to look for her anywhere else.

He spent months obsessing over little details of the meeting. The withering rose petals in her hair, the stray strands of hair playing in the wind, the way her robes bunched at the hem. He was a child, and yet he felt like he'd been with this memory for several years. As a child, he couldn't find any meaning in all of it. But he could string his imagination to the thin strip of the images in his mind and fill in the blanks. He didn't meet Beatrice until later years, but in a way, he didn't need to because she had inspired him to write.

Their next meeting was more formal but just as unforgettable. It happened on the streets of Florence and took him completely by surprise.

He was lost in his thoughts and looking down and he didn't see her approach. She was with her friends, giggling at a joke.

At first, Dante didn't realise that she had called out his name. He kept walking with his head bowed.

Beatrice repeated his name and this time it reached him with the speed and ferocity of a lightning bolt with enough energy to split a tree in half.

It had been so many years since their first meeting. Dante was surprised that Beatrice remembered his name. He looked at her.

She had grown up to be a very beautiful woman. She was wearing a yellow gown. Her hair was tied in a braid around her head and fell loose at the back. Her eyes still had that distinctive spark.

'We haven't met in such a long time,' she said. Dante was struck with the same feeling of that had enveloped him all those years ago. He didn't know how to react. Beatrice was standing before him, awaiting his response but he suddenly found himself tongue-tied.

He tried to speak, but the only sound that came out

of his mouth was a weak growl.

Beatrice frowned, and her smile wavered. Dante looked down again and hurried away before he could embarrass himself further in front of her friends.

He didn't know it then, but this brief encounter would be his last meeting with her.

A few years later, she married into the wealthy Bardi family. Dante was deeply immersed in his studies by then and had responded to the news with a feigned indifference though inside him there was a torrent of feelings waiting to erupt. He was convinced that if he had acted at the right time, he could've courted Beatrice and made her his wife. But somehow, this wasn't entirely plausible because he couldn't ever imagine her as an object that he could possess. Once he had realised that they couldn't be together, Dante had also stopped treating Beatrice as a physical presence. She had transcended his physical needs to become love itself and since it was impossible to hold onto something so ephemeral, Dante was satisfied retaining her in his heart and mind.

Still, the news of her death pierced his mind like a painful dart. Dante opened his eyes and looked into the darkness, almost willing it to conjure up Beatrice's ghost so he could talk to her one last time. As much as he had tried to forget her after his marriage, her shadow continued to haunt him. She had made it impossible for him to connect with Gemma, even when he wanted to because every time he looked at his wife, his mind would replace her face with a hazy image of Beatrice.

Dante didn't know when he fell asleep, but he was soon lost in a dream where he was standing in a green field, surrounded by woods. There was a large tree in the middle of the field, and someone was sitting beneath its shade. She stood up when she saw him. She was wearing a white robe. Her hair was loose and there was a withered rose in her hand.

It was Beatrice. She walked towards him, her robe fluttering in the wind.

'Don't speak. Just listen,' she told him as he parted his lips to speak.

'Baffling that one should remain in love for such a long time without the expectation of anything in return,' she said. 'If only I had known… But then again, I hardly could've done anything. It would've only prolonged your misery.'

She stepped closer to him and took his face in her hands. Beatrice's brilliant green eyes were flecked with shattered images of Dante's tearful face.

'We don't choose whom we fall in love with,' she said. 'I know people think that they have a choice. And yes, to an extent they can decide whom they like more. But these matters are set even before one is born.

'You were always meant to love me, and I was always meant to remain ignorant. It is the only way for you to achieve greatness, and me, immortality,' Beatrice said.

He did not understand what she was saying. But he knew that he had no choice but to listen to her and try to remember her words once he woke up.

'It isn't easy to live, loving someone who doesn't even

acknowledge your existence. After all, love is a kind of madness. It is obsessive and reckless. It doesn't adhere to rules prescribed by society. It makes people do terrible things. It fools them into thinking that sinning is a form of expressing themselves. It is everything wrong with being human and yet it is our only way of salvation,' Beatrice said with a sigh and began to walk away from him. She appeared distraught.

'You have known love in the purest of forms. I hope you never forget it or me. You will go on to do great things in life. You will give love a new definition. You'll place it back on the divine seat where it has been knocked off from because of the disease of lust. You will give people a chance to experience freedom in being alone. You will do everything you're meant to do and even though I won't be there with you, I'll always be imprinted in every word you write. Thank you for loving me, Dante. And being the only one to do that.'

Dante woke up with a start. The lamp had gone out, leaving the room in darkness. He looked around slowly, almost expecting her ghost to emerge from the inky darkness. When nothing happened, and after his laboured breathing had subsided, Dante closed his eyes and prayed to the gods who had made it possible for him to see Beatrice one last time.

He finally understood that he had elevated Beatrice to a place in his mind that was supposed to be occupied by God, and now that she was permanently fixed in the holiest of spots, there was nobody who could replace her.

There wasn't a lot that could be achieved by harbouring unrequited love. Once the physical proof of love was gone, so did its impression until it was just a few faded images. However, Dante knew that he could preserve Beatrice in immortality. He didn't know how to paint or sing, but he knew the power of the written word. If he could sublimate Beatrice in any form of literature, he could save her from being forgotten.

Beauty is perishable. It can be described in words and painted on canvas but nothing in this universe could compare to the images that flicker in one's memory. Those precious moments that one kept safe from being tarnished by the gaze of other people are the only thing that is more sacred than divine powers. Beatrice was just one woman among many on this earth, and like most of them, she would be forgotten because her life hadn't been significant enough to be stored in the books of history. To everyone else, she had been a mortal being who had fulfilled her duties as a daughter, friend and wife. Beatrice would be remembered for all the good and bad she did to her fellow beings, and all the ambiguities of her character would be buried under the weight of binaries that reduced a person to vague finalities. Could he do something different to preserve her as the glorious inspiration she had proved to be for him? His love for her was incomplete, yes, but it was also pure because it hadn't been tainted by the experience of being with her and knowing her intimately. Would he love her as much if she had mirrored his feelings and they had shared each other's desires? He didn't know and would never know. He did know that the idea of loving someone was greater than actually loving them. An idea had infinite possibilities and could be moulded to fit the vision of the creator but when that idea became a reality, its chances of ever transcending its roots in the physical world disappeared.

Dante rifled through the stack of parchment in front of him, pulled one out and laid it out before him. He had to write down all his thoughts so he wouldn't forget them later. His grief at losing Beatrice had pushed him into the abyss of despair but his love for her had pulled him out with a starkly different definition of love itself. When the earthly longing subsided, what remained were the impressions that a person had cast upon the mind of his or her admirer. Dante couldn't resurrect Beatrice's spirit, but he could preserve it. He'd at least try.

Orpheus and Eurydice

Later, when all the efforts had been exhausted, he'd attempt to bring her back by redrawing her in his mind's eye; her dark green eyes, long lashes, bowed lips, and heavy, lustrous red hair. He could make her smile and turn her face to the light. He could deform his memories and create her in the empty spaces.

Eurydice flickered like a feeble flame before him when he was awake, burning bright for a moment before the cruel winds sniffed her out. In his dreams, she was less ethereal, less vacant, but just as elusive. This half-formed, diseased, and static version of her kept repeating itself in his mind as he wandered aimlessly in the valleys of Mount Rhodope during his last days of existence.

This story comes from Greece.

It hadn't been so dismal in the beginning, but there had been plenty of warning signs that he had ignored.

They were married in the shade of a magnificent bower made by the wood naiads. Hymen, holding his torch aloft had led the ceremony. Eurydice had looked radiant in her white robe, her hair spun around her little head in braids. She had been too excited to notice that the God of Marriage had been uncharacteristically mournful, and that the flames had burned indifferently even without the weight of wind upon them.

Orpheus hadn't given it much thought either. Afterward, when she had insisted on playing with the naiads to celebrate their union, he had allowed Eurydice to go as far as the place where the grass grew tall, and the creatures of the underworld practiced with reckless freedom.

Barefoot, her hair loose and flying in the breeze, Eurydice danced with the naiads as Orpheus struck his lyre. The music was at once sensual and pure, flowing among their arched toes, and elegantly stretched arms.

Lost in the trance, she didn't sense the sudden, slippery streak of movement in the grass, as the snake slithered toward her.

She was laughing. She was happy.

Orpheus, looking at his wife's ecstasy was overcome with desire. He got up and walked toward her.

It was then, as he was about to take her in his arms, that the snake opened its terrible mouth and jammed its fangs on Eurydice's ankle.

Eurydice jumped. The grass pulsed as the snake shot back into the dense thicket, its fangs tipped with her blood.

At first, she didn't know what had happened, so she merely looked at Orpheus with a confused expression before she fell down to the ground.

Orpheus looked at her feet, her blanched skin. It was done, and he didn't have much time with her.

'Listen, my love,' Eurydice whispered. 'You must… must remember me, remember our love.'

'Yes, yes, you're my everything. My everything,' Orpheus cried.

Eurydice touched his faced with her cold palm and smiled, her mouth quivering.

Orpheus wanted her to speak; to say that their love had not been in vain; that she'd wait for him even in the underworld. He kept staring at her, seeking just one sign in the twitches of her eyelids, but saw nothing.

Suddenly, her hand dropped and fell lifeless to the side. Her wide eyes relaxed and hardened as a stone. She was dead.

And now, a scene emerged before his tear-filled eyes.

Tendrils of her red hair stuck to his bare shoulders, her fingers tracing a lazy line on his skin. They were sitting on the steps leading up to his house. The sky was a shade of purple, dipped in the orange residue of the sinking sun. Eurydice hadn't let him sleep after making love, insisting that they should sit outside and witness the sunset. She'd been so beautiful then, her eyes shining brightly, and the smell of lilies wafting from her hair.

He'd spent most of the evening just staring at her.

And now, he couldn't bear to look at her at all. She was lying on the ground, her complexion white as marble. Orpheus let out a strangled cry, which came out as a pathetic, enraged wail. He put his arms around her and wept until the naiads had to wrench his firm hold on her body.

When he awoke from his delirium, Orpheus struck a tune so mournful and grief-stricken from his lyre that even the heaven wept for days in sympathy.

Eurydice was gone where he couldn't follow, but Orpheus pledged that he'd crack the gates of hell and bring her back to him.

And so, he bound his lyre to his back and journeyed down to the ghoulish world in search of his wife.

***

The main hall of hell was surprisingly plain. The floor was made of dark granite. It was spotless. Orpheus could see his elongated, warped reflection on the stones. If he had looked closely, he could've seen the scene of his death in them. Instead, he kept walking, his eyes lowered to the ground, till he came upon the couple who ruled the underworld.

The Lady of Hell looked down at him from her throne.

'Speak,' she commanded.

Orpheus looked up. He was stunned by her sheer beauty, and the vehemence with which she addressed him, as if he was a speck of dust that she could blow into oblivion by a careless breath. She was wearing a blue robe. Her pale, angular face shone with a lunar glow. Tendrils of holly were braided in her long, loose hair that touched the floor.

Beside her, Hades looked like he was composed of ashes and despair. While Persephone had retained a sliver of light in her, an eternity in hell had lent her husband's visage the expression of an endless void. His skin was parched and papery, his eyes mere black scratches that seemed full of fury, and his lips appeared on the verge of issuing damnation to the puny human standing below him.

The shadows floating around his seat, seething with the repressed agony of doomed and sinful souls. Their twisted, mangled forms penetrated Orpheus's mind where similar blackened images of Eurydice began to take shape.

He had to do something. He had to save her.

'O gods of this world, placed below the earth, to which all who are created mortals descend! If you allow me, it is lawful, to set aside the fiction of idle tongues and speak the truth, I have not come here to see dark Tartarus, nor to bind Cerberus, Medusa's child, with his three necks, and snaky hair. My wife is the cause of my journey. A viper she trod on, which infused its venom into her body and robbed her of her best years. I longed to be able to accept it, and I do not say I have not tried: Love won.'

Persephone stifled the urge to send a shadow slashing his way and cutting him in half. She had come across plenty of such unrepentant narcissists in the snare of love who thought they could fool death. As if she hadn't tried it herself.

'You ventured down to the underworld, faced our grotesque populous, risked our wrath and yet, you couldn't perform the simplest act of slaying yourself and binding your soul with your beloved for eternity in death, here?' she sneered. 'Such cowardice and hubris shall be punishable with the most horrendous torture.'

And why hadn't he done exactly that? Trapped the snake's thin mouth between his fingers and ingested the same poison that had killed his wife? Then, they would've been fused together forever among the unremarkable wraiths of this lightless realm. But he couldn't do it, to be severed from the worldly joys above. The sulphurous craters of hell seemed to him an even worse fate than they'd already been dealt.

Orpheus bowed his head, and said, 'He is a god well known in the world above, though I do not know if it is so here: though I do imagine him to be here as well, and if the story of that rape in ancient times is not a lie, you also were wedded by Amor. I beg you, by these fearful places, by this immense abyss, and the silence of your vast realms, reverse Eurydice's swift death. All things are destined to be yours, and though we delay a while, sooner or later we hasten home. Here we are all bound, this is our final abode, and you hold the longest reign over the human race. Eurydice, too, will be yours to command when she has lived out her destined span of years. I ask this benefit as a gift; but, if the fates refuse my wife this kindness, I am determined not to return. You can delight in both our deaths.'

Persephone smiled. She was charmed by the fool's confidence and his ability to make himself pathetic. Looking around, she saw the tear-streaked faces of the spirits that had gathered around him, their mild grey figures blurring around his solid, brown and still mortal body.

In the further reaches of hell, Tantalus did not stretch for the ever-retreating water, Ixion's wheel was still, the vultures did not pluck at Tityus' liver, the Belides, the daughters of Danaus, left their water jars, and even Sisyphus was still, perched on his rock.

'So shall it be.'

'No.'

The Lord of Death had been listening intently to the mortal man's dirges. The saccharine details of his love for another worthless human didn't impress him much, but he'd let himself be seduced by his music. It had an ethereal lilt, with the power to expand the boundaries of the worlds.

'You shall have what you desire, mortal,' he said, and saw Persephone dig her nails in the throne's armrest.

'My lord,' she whispered to him. 'The dead cannot be resurrected and sent back to the living world. If you grant his wishes, you will only be encouraging others with the audacity to conquer death itself.'

Hades slowly turned to look at her. He'd seen her angry many times before – her slender body would stiffen, as if she were drawing herself back only to snap at him even more viciously.

'And none shall be brave enough to pass through the jagged passages of this dreaded paradise,' he told her. 'Nor shall they inflict themselves with a feeling so pure and ravaging that would make the monstrous faces of hell crumple up in melancholy. He shall have his wish.'

The slightest trace of smirk on her husband's face both annoyed and frightened Persephone. She knew perfectly well that however much he had been moved by Orpheus' songs, Hades would never let a departed soul leave his clutches. So, what was he going to do with the poor mortal and his wife?

Orpheus, stupefied by Hades' subterranean baritone, was still collecting his thoughts that had scattered by its grim force. Had he heard right? Could he take Eurydice back with him, healed and sewed with her body, or was it a trick that hid its hideous purpose beneath the brocaded skin of beneficence?

'Bring her, then,' Persephone said, in her rasping voice.

The grey mass that had gathered at the edges of the hall began to shift and Eurydice emerged from the fog of shapeless souls, in a distorted image of what she used to be. Her face was devoid of its beautiful features. Her robe was torn and pockmarked in various places, and she lurched toward him, still wincing from the pain of the viper's bite.

Transparent, bloodless and anaemic as she was, Orpheus fell to his knees when he saw her approach and wept openly at the sight of his beloved.

Hades looked at the thin wraith walking toward Orpheus, at the mortal bent and weeping, with the look of a being that was far above such puny emotions. Persephone was still, almost as if she were anticipating a tidal wave of black bile to come rushing into the hall and sweep away the two lovers.

Eurydice stumbled before Orpheus, and with a surge of emotion, he moved forward to try and take her in his arms, only to pass through the transparent form of her reflection.

Hades chuckled. Persephone dug her nails deeper into the armrest, almost cracking their tips.

'If I could walk on burning coals for eons till my feet were mere blisters on the bone, the agony still wouldn't be enough for what I felt when you were snatched from me,' Orpheus said as he wept inconsolably.

Eurydice wanted to speak but she couldn't. Her thoughts were frenzied whirlpools across the flat plain of her mind.

'Why can't you speak?' Orpheus cried. 'Why, my gods, have ye taken her speech and rendered her a mute ghost? How, in this gaseous form, shall I carry her up to the earth?'

'Foolish mortal!' Hades said with a sneer. 'Step away and stop your snivelling or I shall inflict on you with the most vicious of curses.'

Orpheus jumped away from Eurydice and clasped his hands in prayer so as not to offend the god of death anymore.

'My lord, are you certain?' Persephone asked.

'I am,' Hades said. And he raised his arm and commanded the rejuvenation of Eurydice's spirit.

Hades' miracle was swift, and it was as if she'd never left the living world. Eurydice felt her weak outline fill with the vitality of life.

At a loss of words at this miracle, Orpheus could only tremble in the presence of the lucent glow of his wife.

Eurydice stepped forward and took Orpheus' hand in hers.

'If only I had known...' But she couldn't complete her sentence and burst into tears of relief. The lovers embraced each other. Hades, watching the scene with an icy fascination, grew bored and rapped his knuckles on the armrest to separate them from each other.

'Enough!' he bellowed.

'My lord, no bounties and offerings shall be enough to pay the price of the miracle you have bestowed to us!' Orpheus said.

Hades' face was impassive at Orpheus' praises and Persephone could feel his patience wearing thin.

'You both can leave now,' she said. 'Live your life with the knowledge that blessings have a way of turning into curses if mortals stray from their fated paths. You have already insulted death once, Orpheus. It won't be so forgiving the next time it comes for your beloved.'

Hades added, 'As you take her back, mortal, remember that if you turn to look at your beloved's face while you're still in the shade of my world, I will take her back, and she will be bound to my realm for eternity.'

Persephone stifled a laugh. It was never that easy. Hades could never let anyone walk into his world and take what was his. He had read Orpheus' nature and twisted his miracle to extend the mortal's agony. It was awful, but then again, gods were seldom known to be kind.

'Yes, my gods,' Orpheus said. 'I shall never……'-

'Go away, now,' Hades said irritably. 'Get out of my palace before I change my mind and bury you both under my feet!'

Orpheus took Eurydice's hand in his, turned around and walked away.

They walked upward, Orpheus staring ahead into the darkness, trying to discern any lurking danger, and Eurydice behind him, following.

'When we reach the surface, I shall devote my living days to your service,' said Eurydice

'No, I shall be the one to serve you,' Orpheus said, kicking a stone away. 'You have suffered enough in this unforgiving lightless place.'

After a while, as the path became unruly and strewn with even more debris that the underground had absorbed from above, their conversation became less constant, and in the haste to reach to the top, Orpheus was quiet.

Finally, after what seemed like ages, it seemed that they were near the top. Orpheus could feel the feet of humans thumping on earth above him. He quickened his pace.

They were so close. So close. A few more steps and then they'd be together again. Orpheus was agitated.

Eurydice's footsteps had become softer as they had ascended and now doubt crept into his mind.

What if she wasn't behind him? What if Hades had played a trick on him and replaced his wife with a demoness who could mimic her voice and fool him into believing her? What if he had brought along someone else by mistake?

No, he couldn't lose her again. He wouldn't.

He could see the circular arc of light at the end. If he could just take a glimpse as they reached the threshold, he'd be assured of her presence.

And thus, just as they were about to exit the realm of the dead, Orpheus turned to look at his beloved.

A blur of flesh and flapping cloth, a feeble, stunned cry and then nothing as Eurydice was snatched back into the underworld leaving Orpheus alone at the edge of the gate.

What had he done? Why had he turned to look?

Orpheus crumpled into a tearful heap on the ground, shaking and screaming to the gods to come and help him. But it was no good. What was done was done. Eurydice was gone and there was no other way to reach her. Orpheus beat the ground with his hands until they bled.

Mad with grief, he was left adrift in the mortal world. Without his Eurydice, nothing could satiate him.

His music had lost its lustre and never did his lyre play a tune that could please the ear of its listener.

Death had won in the end and severed two lovers across two planes of existence, the boundaries of which would never become porous again.

Dushyant and Shakuntala

She'd been threading a garland, pushing one marigold flower down the needle after another, and staring at the tangle of foliage.

It was cool in the forest. She'd cleaned the ground around her and was sitting on a mat made of nettles and leaves. This was her favourite spot to sit and work. She had discovered it by accident. One day, while out with her pet deer, Kaushal, she spotted a circular patch of land surrounded by giant elm trees. It looked like someone had created it specifically to build a hut but had changed his mind. Surveying the space, Shakuntala was mystified as to what had led the stranger to abandon it. The trees were strong, with strong bark and towering branches that

---

This story comes from India.

seemed to form a canopy to protect one from the sun's glare. She walked around the circle, looking for traps and any danger that might startle or attack her. And when she was assured that the place held no danger, she decided to make it her own for work and respite.

But that day, Shakuntala was feeling peculiarly exposed. As if there were elements in the forest that were watching her. She knew that King Dushyant had arrived in the forest for the royal hunt, and his followers would be moving around, looking for fresh game. Fearing that Kaushal might run away and fall victim to their arrows, Shakuntala had left her pet at the hermitage.

Still, the work had to be done. Shakuntala sat in the imposing silence of the woods and continued to thread the garland.

She returned to the hermitage later in the afternoon, carrying the garlands in a basket and felt the stirrings of change. The air was redolent with sweat and churned earth. She also felt the lingering smell of blood and torn flesh.

'Did the men from the king's army take refuge here?' she asked Ambala, her friend, as she set the basket down on the ground.

'Yes, the king was chasing a deer,' Ambala said, 'He came here for just a moment, before going in search again. I believe he will come again after he his hunt.'

Shakuntala clapped her hands to brush away the dirt and dipped them in the basin of water nearby.

'We shouldn't let them inside after their violent revelries,' she told Ambala. 'The King and his men should know that this is a sacred place for us. It shouldn't be open to killers of living things.'

Ambala scratched her nose. 'Aren't all human beings the killers of living things in one way or another? Where do we draw the line that should not be crossed when it comes to atrocities against people and animals?'

Shakuntala didn't know how to answer her questions, or if they even had answers. She resented Ambala's calm demeanour and her astute observations. Her friend had been born with a mind that was sensitive to reality, while Shakuntala had always been vulnerable to daydreams and often drifted away into the realm of fanciful thoughts. Surprisingly, their differing world views and nature never clashed or cause any friction between them.

Shakuntala took Ambala's hand and stood up. They busied themselves with the daily chores.

They spent almost the entire afternoon in the garden that they tended. Shakuntala dug the earth while Ambala sprinkled sunflower seeds. They were trying to find a way to prop up a slim string of grapevine and were having difficulty in twisting the stubborn tendril around the pole. Suddenly, the thunderous approach of hoofs and spirited laugh of the soldiers broke the quiet of their abode. The soldiers hurried toward the hermitage.

'Oh, here they come again,' Shakuntala muttered. 'Let's go and see what they want.'

'But the elders would frown upon it,' Ambala said. 'And I don't think it'd be very wise to join the company of men who have just come from the hunt.'

Shakuntala didn't understand the logic of her friend's argument. She didn't feel any sense of danger in facing a few tired men who'd just come back after killing defenceless creatures. She wanted to see the arrogance on their faces and ask them the reason for such glee when all they'd achieved was the murder of god's creation.

Before Ambala could protest further, Shakuntala left the garden and went straight to the group of men congregated at the entrance of the hermitage, with a ragtag bunch of commoners behind them.

'Can you provide water to us poor men?' one of the soldiers asked when he saw her approach them.

'Where's your water? Drink that instead,' Shakuntala wanted to say but looking at the commoners in the corner, who looked harassed and tired, she nodded and went back to get a pot from her hut.

When she came back, most of the soldiers had dispersed, and the only ones left were the commoners. She noticed that a relatively clean and good-looking man had joined the group.

'Where did everyone go?' she asked him. 'Don't they feel thirsty any longer?'

'They went back to the king, my lady,' the man said, bowing his head.

Shakuntala frowned. The man standing before her seemed too respectful and serene to be a commoner.

He was tall, with broad shoulders and a muscular chest. His thick, dark hair was slicked back in a simple style that made him look sober and handsome. He had almond brown eyes, a straight nose and full lips.

He was beautiful and had an aura of authority around him that she had never seen before in a man. Maybe he was a scholar. There was something very different about him. He didn't look at her the way some other men did. His gaze, while enamoured by her beauty, remained respectful and non-threatening.

'Who are you?' Shakuntala asked him suddenly and regretted it.

The man only smiled and knelt down to drink the water she offered.

Shakuntala poured water into his cupped hands, and he took a few gulps. He drew his palms along his hair, patting them into place. Stray droplets of water slipped down from his lips, clung lightly to his chin and then trailed down his neck. Shakuntala found herself desiring him in a way she had never thought possible.

'I am Dushyant, the King of Hastinapur, my lady.'

Shakuntala was shocked and relieved at the same time.

'Why should I believe you?' she asked him. 'Why would the King of Hastinapur come to the hermitage in the guise of a common man? Or was this a trick to test the honourable and simple people for some petty reason?'

Dushyant chuckled. 'I didn't intend to mock you, my lady. I had entered this hermitage in the search of an escaped deer, but sage Vaikhānasa forbade me from slaying it because it belonged to the people of this place. I was just looking around when I saw you approaching me with a pot of water. Since I was thirsty, I couldn't decline such kindness.'

Shakuntala wasn't convinced. Dushyant had a good reputation as a king. He was just and kind, as every king should be if he wanted a long and peaceful rule. But he could be intensely violent as well. She had heard frightening stories about his conquests that made him seem like an ever-morphing shadow that would creep up on people and deform them at his will. She'd always shrugged at such tales, believing them to be made up only to give the king a legendary status. But the truth was that nobody could anticipate the sudden swings of the mind of such a powerful man. Who knew what storms raged under the surface of his placid face.

'My Lord, forgive me for doubting you,' she said even though every particle in her being screamed that she shouldn't apologise because she was not wrong in doubting him at all. 'I understand that you are tired. But I brought this pot of water for your men, who were standing just where you're standing now. They looked like they needed help. And now they're gone. Did you send them away?'

She made herself sound amenable, careful not to make him mad, but she couldn't let him go away without telling her about the fate of the men.

Dushyant smiled. 'I asked them to join the others at the end of the path where I have arranged food and drinks for them.'

Shakuntala wanted to tell him that the forest wasn't one of his elaborately designed dining halls where he could hold grand dinners, but she refrained from saying anything objectionable. He was the king after all, and it was likely that the ground she was standing on belonged to him as well.

But that doesn't mean he can do what he wants whenever he wants, Shakuntala thought.

'I understand that, my lord,' she said. 'I hope your men will keep the dignity of the hermitage in mind and restrain themselves from disturbing the peace of this holy place.'

'I have told them to keep their enthusiasm in check,' Dushyant said. 'I was hoping you'd help me explore the hermitage.'

The glint in his eyes told Shakuntala that she shouldn't decline his request. If it was a request at all. She took him to the garden.

Dushyant seemed impressed with their labours and nodded appreciatively at the curling vines, and rows of marigolds, roses, violets, and peonies. He moved his fingers along their fragile heads and turned over the petals and pressed the thumb on the growing buds.

'I believe your palace has a better garden,' said Shakuntala, watching Dushyant as he teased apart the petals of a delicate hibiscus. They had been together only for a short time but she felt herself being drawn to him as if pulled by an invisible string that was getting stronger with every passing minute. She wanted to catch him in moments when he wasn't aware of her presence so that she could get to know the kind of person he was without the weight of royalty on him.

Her gaze traced the firm movements of his fingers as

they pressed and flicked the petals. His touch was gentle, as if he knew his strength could tear them apart and kept it in check.

'This would look beautiful in your hair,' King Dushyant said suddenly and turned to look at her with an expectant expression. 'Will the lady give me permission to decorate her tresses?'

Shakuntala hesitated. She couldn't possibly agree to King Dushyant's request. The hermitage was not a place to initiate romance, and she knew all about the restless hearts of kings who promised their love to one woman while courting several others at the same time. She wouldn't become one of his conquests.

'What are you suggesting, my lord?' she asked in a challenging tone. 'Did you ask me to show you around just for a game of seduction and then be on your way? Let me tell you now so you won't have any doubts later on. I may be poor and defenceless but you can't take away my dignity by offering me such sweetened gifts and compliments.'

Dushyant looked as if he was about to explode into uncontrolled rage. His lips began to curl into a sneer, and his eyes narrowed But then just as suddenly, his face returned to its neutral expression.

'You mistake my chivalry for lechery, my lady,' he said. 'If I wanted to, I could have you for myself here and now. But no, such barbarism is not the way of kings. I just believed that the flower would suit the contours of your hair.'

They were dancing around in circles and reaching nowhere. It was infuriating to talk to someone you knew had all the power so you could never completely oppose him or refuse to submit to his desires. Shakuntala wanted Dushyant to be hers, but she couldn't give herself away fully or lose herself either.

'I'm just not used to talking to the King of Hastinapur in a casual tone. You may not act like it, but your presence can be overwhelming,' she said. 'I apologise for doubting you again. You may put the flower in my hair.'

As he got closer to her, Shakuntala could smell the sweet, earthy fragrance of sandalwood that emanated from Dushyant's person. His fingers unravelled the knots in her hair. He gathered her loose tresses in his hand, his fingers almost touching the skin of her neck. A bolt of desire rushed through Shakuntala's body as his hand grazed against her bare skin.

After he was done beautifying her, Dushyant told her to turn around and look at him. The setting sun had washed the sky in crimson. It seemed to her that they'd been together for days. Somehow, even though she didn't know anything about King Dushyant, Shakuntala believed that he had revealed more of himself to her than to any person in his palace.

She looked at him, and a tear escaped from the corner of her eye. Dushyant took her in his arms, and Shakuntala confessed her love for him in teary, breathless whispers.

Afterward, Dushyant told her that the ministers at the palace might disapprove of their match, and if they wanted to stay together, they should get married without the knowledge of the elders before they could put a wrench in their plans.

Shakuntala wasn't opposed to Gandharva vivaah. She trusted Dushyant and knew that he'd accept her as his wife once he got back to the palace. They were married a few days later, in private and made love at Shakuntala's secret spot.

Their days of happiness were numbered. As Dushyant had to go back to the capitol to take care of the affairs of the country. He had to leave his wife alone at the hermitage until he could find a good time to announce their union to the world. Shakuntala didn't oppose his decision but asked for some evidence through which she could prove that they were man and wife. As a token of remembrance, Dushyant presented her with his signet ring and asked her to present it to him at the court. He would remember her and give her the rightful place beside him.

Shakuntala felt like a chunk of her soul had been cut out from her body when Dushyant departed the hermitage. She started to spend her time thinking of the moment when she'd be reunited with her husband. Ambala noticed her friend's emotional turmoil and tried to convince her that Dushyant would call for her at the right moment. While she understood and even appreciated Ambala's efforts to alleviate her mood, she just couldn't let go of the lingering doubts that the separation had caused. What would she do if Dushyant refused to acknowledge her? She'd not be able to face her elders at the hermitage and would have to leave the sanctuary of the forest for an unknown place where she'd have to live in infamy forever. There was no place on earth for women who had given themselves to men who didn't want them later. The Gandharva marriage had no witnesses. And even the ring that Dushyant had given her would be seen as an object of theft if he didn't recognise her.

Her mind was tortured with doubts making it impossible for her to focus on her work. She would sit outside her hut and think about the day when she'd be reunited with her husband.

One fateful day, Shakuntala's mind was lost in thoughts about the king, when the revered rishi Durvasa came to her hut and stood before her in expectation of attendance. But Shakuntala, lost in her thoughts, didn't see him standing at the foot of the hermitage steps.

Durvasa was blind with anger.

'Stupid girl,' he bellowed. 'How dare you disrespect me!'

Shakuntala was jerked back to reality. She looked at Durvasa's enraged visage and fell to her knees.

'Forgive me, forgive me, Shri Durvasa,' she cried. 'I didn't mean to disrespect you.'

But Durvasa's anger could not be appeased.

'You dare to insult me and then ask for my forgiveness?' he roared. 'I will not let your audacity go without punishment. I curse you that the being you were fantasising about will forget you forever. You shall remain a blot of darkness in his mind, nothing else.'

Shakuntala looked at the sage, pale with fear. Ambala rushed to the scene and fell at Durvasa's feet.

'Shri Durvasa, please forgive her,' she pleaded. 'Her mind has been confused since her husband went away. They couldn't spend much time together and she has been lost in dreams about him. Your curse will wrench the two souls forever and even the gods will weep at this injustice to them.'

'I never intended to insult you, Shri Durvasa,' Shakuntala wept. 'It was my ill fortune that I happened to be in a state of trance when you appeared and failed to acknowledge you. I will do any penance. I will read the scriptures till my dying day. Please take back this curse.'

Durvasa was prone to anger, but he wasn't cruel. Looking at the two women kneeling before him, his anger was somewhat appeased.

'I can't take the curse back. It is impossible to do so. However, I can offer you a way around it,' Durvasa said.

Shakuntala looked at him with hope. She was trembling, unable to control the emotions that were threatening to overwhelm her.

'Do you have an object that was gifted to you by your husband?' Durvasa asked.

'Yes, I have the signet ring he gave me before departing,' Shakuntala said. 'He told me to present it to him when we meet so he could remember me.'

Durvasa inspected the signet ring. So, this girl had married the King of Hastinapur. He had heard tales of the king's greatness and knew that he wouldn't abandon Shakuntala in the hermitage after marrying her. He would accept his wife once she showed him the ring.

'Take this, child,' Durvasa said in a gentler tone. 'Show this to your husband when you meet him, and he will remember everything about you in an instant.'

Shakuntala didn't know how to thank the sage for his kindness. She had been punished for her ignorance but had found a way to get out of the curse.

To further atone for her mistakes, she attended to sage Durvasa during his entire stay at the hermitage. But as days went by and there was no news from Dushyant, she began to get increasingly agitated. Their brief encounter seemed like a dream to her now. It had been so beautiful, but like many beautiful things, it was fragile and didn't have the strength to last.

She would've taken it as the decision of the divine powers that she did not deserve to be happy, if she hadn't realised that she was pregnant with Dushyant's child.

'I'll go with you to the palace,' Ambala said, when Shakuntala that she was going to meet the king. 'We will meet King Dushyant together. He has to accept you and his child who'll be coming into this world soon.'

Shakuntala didn't have much hope, but she had to try and convince Dushyant for the sake of their child. She agreed to travel with Ambala to the capital. They took the blessing of the sages and left for the city with a group of women who'd be spreading the word of God among the citizens.

Their journey was arduous and Shakuntala was often overwhelmed with grief and tiredness. But she knew that she had to reach the palace and meet Dushyant as soon as possible before she started showing her pregnancy.

One day, the tired group took refuge by the banks of a river. Enchanted by its youthful, and vigorous flow, even Shakuntala joined her friends to play in the churning water.

She didn't know the exact moment when it happened. She had been wearing the signet ring because she was afraid of losing it if she kept it anywhere else. One moment, her hand was under the water, feeling the cold, restless current flowing between her fingers, and when she raised it again, the ring had slipped away, pulled by the force of the torrent.

Nothing had prepared her for this tragedy. Shakuntala wailed in frustration and agony until Ambala had to stop her lest she hurt her unborn child.

Shakuntala knew that her last chance to reunite with Dushyant had gone with the signet ring. And yet, she entered the palace that day, hoping that her husband still remembered her. She believed that if nothing else, her love for him was resilient enough to remain untouched by the suffocating shroud of the curse.

'I don't remember you, my lady,' Dushyant told her, gently but firmly, when she asked if he recognised her.

'How can you forget our time together?' Shakuntala asked. She was no longer sobbing. Tears were of no use to her anymore. She had cried and begged the gods to reverse her misfortune but to no avail. Love was not a crime. It was salvation. And if she were to be denied the promise of ever finding it again, she'd face her fate with dignity, she decided.

'No, my lady,' Dushyant said. 'I believe that you

have mistaken me for someone else. I hope you find your loved one.'

His voice hadn't lost its deep but gentle texture, and he looked much the same. His eyes were still bright and alert. But the way he looked at her was very different. There was no recognition, no affection in his gaze. Just concern for a wayward woman who had mistaken him for her husband.

Shakuntala couldn't make her love bring back his memory. She had lost, and Durvasa's curse had won. She had to accept defeat.

'Yes, my king, I seem to be looking for a man who is no longer here,' she said. 'Thank you for extending your help, but I don't think even you could find him. I'll take my leave now.'

Shakuntala didn't have the courage to tell the truth to the sages. So upon returning, she quietly left the hermitage and built a hut in the forest. She gave birth to her son with Ambala assisting her and named him Bharata.

Years passed, and as Bharata grew up, Shakuntala became more involved in his education. Shorn of her romanticism and dreams, she was a changed woman. She lived only for her child and hoped that he'd grow up to be a good, and kind man.

Meanwhile, Dushyant continued to rule his kingdom in peace. He was alone. He had long given up worrying about himself and lived only to serve his subjects. He didn't mind being without a wife.

However, all that changed the day he saw the signet

ring. A fish had swallowed it when it had slipped from Shakuntala's finger and found its way into the hands of an honest fisherman when he caught the fish. He took it to the palace to have it examined as he felt it belonged to the king.

'I believe that you might be looking for it, sire,' the fisherman said.

Dushyant picked up the ring and was instantly flooded with visions from the past. Shakuntala's beauty had teased him in his dreams for years. He remembered everything about his wife. How he had courted her, married her, and left her in the forest. He realised she had come to claim her place beside him and he had rejected her.

He sprang to his feet and told everyone that the court was adjourned for the day. He left for the forest almost immediately and went straight to the hermitage to find his wife.

'She doesn't live here anymore, my king,' Ambala told him when he asked her about Shakuntala's whereabouts. He could sense a coldness in Ambala's voice, which signified that he was too late.

'Where did she go then, I hope she didn't…' Dushyant couldn't bring himself to voice his terrible thought.

'No, she did not take her own life,' Ambala said, no longer acting the part of a timid subject of the king. Seeing the sincerity in his face, she added, 'She lives in a hut deep in the forest, with her son.'

Her son? Their son? What else had he missed? Dushyant looked up to the heavens and willed them to fall punishment on him for his terrible mistake that had ruined two innocent lives.

'Will you take me to her?' Dushyant said.

Ambala looked at the King of Hastinapur and realised that she had never seen an expression so pathetic and sorrowful in her life.

She agreed to take him to Shakuntala but warned her that his wife was a different woman now.

***

Shakuntala was watching Bharata play in the yard. Her hands were busy threading a garland for the deities. It was afternoon, but not too hot. She was lost in her work and didn't have any disturbing thoughts fluttering around in her mind.

Suddenly, she heard Bharata cry out and looked up. He was jumping around excitedly, pointing at a new arrival.

'Ambala,' Shakuntala said, confused. 'Is everything alright, why do you look like this?'

Dushyant was standing beside her. He hadn't changed much in five years. But the way he looked at her, Shakuntala felt that with the passage of time, he appeared to have aged by several decades.

She had to hold on to the door to steady herself.

'Who is this, mother?' Bharata cried. 'Who did Ambala didi bring?'

Shakuntala didn't answer him, couldn't answer him. Her mind had been stripped clean of every explanation except the flickering images of the day when she had first seen Dushayant standing outside the hermitage in the guise of a common man. She hadn't thought about it then, but now she was certain that she had fallen in love with him at the moment she'd laid her eyes on him.

Now, as he walked toward her, and stretched his arms out to embrace her, Shakuntala's eyes filled with tears. She hadn't cried in a long time because tears had become futile. She had given up on love, thinking that she had been punished for transgressing the rules of the world in desiring a king. She had tried to forget him because she had believed the curse would remain unbroken until the day she died.

But here he was, so close to her. His eyes shone with tears as well. He remembered her. He remembered everything.

As the lovers embraced, their child cheered and clapped. He didn't know their story or the reason behind the sadness that inflected this moment of happiness, but he had seen their tearful smiles, and the way they seemed to melt into each other, and he knew in his heart that they belonged together.

Tristan and Isolde

The sea was unpredictable. Mysterious and unfathomable. It was vast and deep and contained creatures and horrors that were yet to be discovered. The waves surged and sighed with such violent force that Isolde was scared they'd cut into the ship and rip it into shreds. She was standing at the edge of the pier, staring at the orange curve of the sun as it sank farther into the sea. The world seemed to tilt if she stared long enough at the thin line of the horizon. As if everything just fell away, slipping into grey nothingness without much fuss, simply vanishing after a point. Isolde liked that, but she knew it wasn't possible. The sea stretched for miles and miles, covering the earth and whatever gliding monsters existed in its depths.

This story comes from England.

'My lady, are you ready to board now?'

Isolde nodded slowly, still staring ahead.

'Do you feel burdened, Mira?' she asked her handmaid, walking behind her.

'Burdened by what, my lady?'

'Everything,' Isolde said. 'Burdened by me. The soldier who ogles at you. The crown that forces you to take care of me. The family you can't wait to return to but who also expect you to send your wages to them.'

Mira was silent for a moment. She was uncertain if the truth would hurt Isolde or send her into a rage.

'I do what I have to do to survive in this world,' she said.

'Precisely,' Isolde said. She walked back to the ship as if nothing had happened.

Isolde's ability to be so sensitive and aloof at the same time always astonished Mira. She could be stoic and introspective one moment, and the next she'd be berating her maids for failing to do their duties. She was volatile and confused, unable to get out of herself and see things for what they really were in reality. She wanted to see herself as the only one suffering the misfortunes of being a woman while she ignored everyone who even indicated to having similar feelings. Young people could never really see past themselves. Especially, the young royals.

Mira smiled to herself and followed the princess to the ship.

They were about to set sail and there was a lot of commotion on the deck. Isolde had insisted on remaining above deck because she wanted to bid farewell to her home. She didn't have any sentimental attachment to it. In fact, she had hated the cold halls of the castle and the parched gardens that refused to flourish even after titanic efforts by the keepers of the grounds. Her feverish dreams had taunted her with a place that overflowed with lush and opulent halls where she could walk barefoot on the warm ground and appreciate the beauty around her without being interrupted by the silly maids and orders from her father to fulfil her duties.

Isolde detested being a royal princess but she could not imagine her life as a commoner either. She liked the luxury and comfort that came with being a princess, but the responsibilities gave her a severe headache. She wanted to be free, but she didn't want to walk the dirty streets. Her parents wanted her to be perfect while all she wanted was to lounge on her bed and gossip with her friends.

Why had she even agreed to marry King Mark? She knew nothing about him and had little hope of ever loving him. These unions were made out of political necessities. There were no feelings involved. She was expected to perform her duties as a wife and queen and bear children to continue their lineage. It was a prison and there was no way out of it.

Isolde scowled at the sea and her knuckles white as she held on to the railing. The noise behind was making her skin prickle but she held on to her composure. Everyone was busy with their work. They probably wouldn't notice if she slipped over the railing and into the ocean. Her slender body would slash the churning waters, going down in an arc as furious bubbles gathered around her until her clothes would drag her down into the bluish depths. She'd like that.

'I fear you'd snap in half, the way you're holding yourself. Drowning would feel like your lungs are on fire.'

Isolde blinked and caught herself as she leaned almost halfway over the railing. She flinched and stepped back. She had almost stumbled and fell over but a pair of strong arms snatched her back.

'I wasn't planning on jumping,' Isolde said haughtily. She stepped away and looked at her saviour.

He was tall, and blonde with brilliant blue eyes, a straight nose and a strong jawline. He was wearing a knight's armour and a gold chain around his neck. He was strikingly handsome, Isolde would never say it out loud.

'Yes, my lady,' he said. 'But you were standing too close to the edge and could've easily tipped over if somebody had startled you.'

He was looking at her directly as if he knew that she was lying and wanted her to know in return that he was willing to play along with her false tale.

'You did startle me,' she said.

'I apologise, my lady,' he replied. 'It was the only way to bring you out of your reverie.'

Reverie. That had a nice sound to it.

'What's your name?' she asked him.

'I'm Tristan, my lady,' he said. 'I've been tasked with

accompanying you to your future abode.'

'Future abode, eh,' Isolde repeated venomously. 'You could say a prisoner is being transferred to another location to serve her life sentence.'

'If only all prisons had velvet beds and morning tea,' Tristan said.

Isolde hadn't expected him to respond to her comment. She'd never met anyone who dared to banter with her.

'I know,' she said. 'And I would still prefer a watery grave to being handled like a vapid doll who can't move from her place because the pleats of her skirts would get ruffled.'

Tristan nodded and gestured with his hand to the railing.

'I'll distract everyone else,' he said. 'You will have five minutes. Do it now, and I'll spread it around that it was a tragic accident.'

Isolde was shocked by his audacity. Tristan was telling her to jump into the sea and kill herself. His demeanour didn't betray any hint of irony which meant he sincerely wanted her to kill herself if that's what she wanted. Or he was very good at playing mind games and knew she'd never have the gumption to do it. Did he just trick her into making a fool of herself or did he want her to break free?

She appraised him again. Tristan's eyes had a rare clarity that felt as if one could see all the emotions brimming inside them. Isolde was scared of looking into his eyes for too long because she knew she'd be lost forever trying to sift through their mysteries.

'No,' she said, shaking herself away from the moment. 'I value your concern for my happiness, but I can't let my family down by killing myself. They'd have to live with the humiliation of my suicide all their lives. It could also lead to friction between the two empires. All I have to do is marry King Mark, who seems a very remarkable man, and then fulfil my duties as his wife. It isn't as difficult as I imagine it to be. I've seen my mother do it.'

Tristan bowed his head.

'Apologies, my lady,' he said. 'I was mistaken. I did hope you wouldn't take my suggestion to heart. I will make certain that you reach your destination without any difficulty. I will take my leave now.'

'Wait,' Isolde said. 'Will you stay with me through the journey? I don't think I'll be able to make it to the English shores without someone wise by my side.'

'My lady, I just advised you to jump in the sea. I don't think I'm the wisest person to be around you.'

'You didn't mean any harm,' Isolde said. 'I like that you speak your mind without fear of censure or punishment. Our troubles would be way less if people stood up for themselves.'

Isolde was lying. She wasn't particularly bothered by her fickle mind and its whims anymore. She just wanted to spend time with Tristan. She wanted to know him and talk to him about things she'd never told anyone. Somehow, during their brief encounter, she had learnt to trust him more than any of her maids.

Tristan smiled. 'You praise me too much, my lady. I don't

deserve it. However, I shall always stay with you through this journey and you won't be disappointed at my service.'

The ship set sail and Isolde insisted that she spend most of the time on the deck with everyone else. She didn't want to look petulant and royal. Her demands weren't as drastically different from anybody else's so why should she get special treatment? Of course, that wasn't the only reason why she had decided to stay above.

As a personal guard to Isolde, Tristan had to watch out for any sign of danger on the high seas. Isolde was amused by this, considering that there wasn't any apparent danger of pirates, and they would be in Cornwall soon. And although she was touched by his dedication, Isolde wondered if he was focusing on protecting her because he didn't want to talk to her. She couldn't just go and chat with him while he looked like he was about to draw his sword and slash through a pack of enemies.

'He is too serious,' Mira said to her as they were having their evening tea on the deck. Tristan was standing beside Captain Ralph, his back straight and his gaze fixed on the purple horizon.

'He's just doing his duty,' Isolde said.

'Yes, but I don't see anything approaching us,' Mira said. 'He could sit and rest for a bit.'

She was right. Tristan was overdoing it and she had to stop him.

'When you're finished, go tell him I want to talk to him about something,' she told Mira.

Mira nodded. She put her teacup on the table, dabbed

her lips with her kerchief and left. Isolde watched her speaking to Tristan. His eyes registered the information, and he tilted his head to look in her direction as if baffled by her order to meet him. Still, he bowed his head and followed Mira to where Isolde was sitting.

'I fear you'd snap in half if you held yourself upright any longer,' she said, smiling.

Tristan blushed but composed himself immediately.

'I was just doing…'

'Your duty. Yes, yes. But I can't have you stand erect like an automaton every day. Sit and have tea with me.'

Tristan blanched. He lowered his eyes and pursed up his lips as if she'd told him to drink rat poison.

'What is it? You don't want to have a cup of tea with the future queen?' she asked with the slightest edge to her voice.

'No, no it's nothing like that,' Tristan said. 'I don't think everyone else will approve that a guard is having tea with the princess while others have been left out even though they have been working just as hard as me, if not more.'

Isolde smirked. 'You will make a kinder woman of me,' she said and stood up. 'Mira, please distribute tea to every crew member and make sure they get sweets as well. As for you, Hon'ble Tristan, let's take a turn about the deck.'

She held out her hand to Tristan. He took it gently and helped her stand up.

'You seem to be afraid of something,' Isolde said, as

they walked. 'Too cautious, as if you're already afraid of the consequences of something that hasn't happened yet.'

Tristan caught the insinuation in her voice but chose to ignore it.

'I'm not afraid, my lady.' he said. 'But I have always stayed away from temptations of any kind.'

He said the word temptation archly, looking askance at her. Isolde felt the flush spread across her throat. She'd known that Tristan liked her but was keeping himself away to see if she liked him as well.

'Some temptations should be satiated in time,' she said, 'otherwise they turn to regrets.'

'Temptations can lead to sinful actions,' Tristan said. 'Is it worth being godless just to indulge one's desires?'

'Love isn't a sin,' Isolde said in a steely voice. 'It leads to ruin only if it remains unrealised. There is nothing sadder in this world than a man who wakes up late to find all that could've been possible is now far beyond his reach.'

Tristan stopped abruptly and looked straight into her eyes.'And what about King Mark?' he asked. 'He's going to be your husband. Don't you feel any sense of loyalty to him?'

'I don't know him at all,' Isolde said. 'There is no possibility of love between us. It's you I want. And if you agree, we can continue our relationship. Nobody has to know.'

The light in Tristan's eyes blazed brighter.

'Do you know there's a seer on this ship?' he asked

Isolde. 'He claims to know the future of all the men here.'

Isolde was confused by Tristan's statement. Why did he bring up an irrelevant seer into the conversation? Was he so eager to find out about his future?

'I don't understand what you mean,' Isolde said.

'I want you to meet him,' Tristan said. 'I think he has the thing I'm looking for.'

'What are you looking for?'

'Love.'

Isolde followed Tristan to the other end of the deck where she saw a group of men lying flat on the floor with their hands clasped over their chests.

'Who are these people?' she asked Tristan.

'Civilians and workers,' Tristan said. 'They don't get treated to tea and snacks.'

Isolde rolled her eyes but refrained from snapping at him.

'Where is he?' she asked him tersely.

Tristan silently pointed to a thin, blonde man lying in the corner.

'Well, wake him up,' she said, getting irritated by his show of secrecy.

Tristan went to the man and shook him awake.

Isolde squinted, trying to get a better look at the man.

Oh, he is hideous, Isolde thought as the man stood up and slapped his buttocks. Tristan whispered something in his ear that made him smirk. The man didn't look like he could tell the hour of day by looking at the clock and she was supposed to believe that he could tell her future.

Isolde scoffed, ready to reprimand Tristan as they both approached her.

'What....' She began but was stopped halfway.

'My lady, you're still uncertain about your feelings so I hope to provide you a solution,' he said.

Isolde was taken aback and furious. How dare he talk to her like that?

'I'd like you to not presume to know my feelings,' She told him tartly. 'I was hoping to meet a gentleman, but you seem to have little regard when talking to the future queen and I shall have you...'

'Apologies, my lady,' Elgorn said and inclined his head in a faux bow. Isolde wanted to punch him.

'You're not forgiven, and I'll have some words with the king's army regarding you when we depart. Men like you seem to think that they can get away with insulting women just because they have the illusion of superior sex in society. But make no mistake, I'm just as ruthless as any man and I'm going to make sure that you pay for your insolence.'

Elgorn looked as if he had aged a decade as she spoke. He winced and cleared his throat.

'I have the love potion,' he said.

'What?'

'I have the love potion that will confirm your feelings for Tristan. Yes, I know you're in love with him, but you also doubt yourself. Once you take this potion, you'll be able to understand your inner-most emotions clearly and be able to accept your feelings without guilt. I am here to help you, my lady, because I know your destiny does not comply with being the wife of King Mark. When I saw you conversing with Tristan, I knew that you'd found the true love of your life. I was hesitant to interfere, but Tristan's conscious efforts to keep distance from you meant that your love would never be realised if I didn't interfere. That's why I talked to him last night and said that if you confess your love to him today, he should bring you to me. Now that you're here I must tell you that the path ahead for you two won't be easy. King Mark is a kind man, but he will not be happy to discover that you love someone else. Your relationship will result in a great conflict, but I assure you it'd be worth the trouble because in the end, your love will triumph and endure.'

Isolde's mind was reeling. She didn't know if she wanted to believe Elgorn or punish him for transgressing into her private life.

'And what if I don't drink the potion?' she asked. 'What if this is just one of your tricks? I don't know who you are. You certainly can't claim to have my best interests at heart, considering I didn't even treat you like a human being on this ship while I enjoyed all the worldly pleasures. So, what do you get out of my union with Tristan?'

'I don't want anything, my lady,' Elgorn said. 'I just told you the truth. And I don't care much about worldly pleasures. They are not a part of my destiny.'

He was either a maniac or a truly powerful man who had not yet been corrupted by the evil forces that ravaged even the purest of souls on earth. Either way, his knowledge was as dangerous as it was vital.

Isolde had always felt that knowledge about one's own life was confining. The truth didn't set you free, it only gripped your ankle tighter and tighter as you tried to jerk yourself from its grasp.

'Okay, I will drink your love potion,' she told Elgorn. 'I hope you know what you're doing. Tristan, if I die, kill this man, and parade his body...'

'I'm taking the potion with you,' Tristan said. 'I know that I love you, but I want to strengthen that feeling till it is the only thing I know and remember when I look at you.'

Isolde was visibly moved by Tristan's words. She smiled and took his hand in hers.

'Together, then,' she said.

Elgorn handed a flask to Isolde that he had magically conjured into his hands. Isolde took a deep breath and emptied half the potion down her throat. She gave the flask to Tristan, who did the same.

She had expected to feel different after taking the potion, but she didn't experience any change. Tristan frowned, and she realised that he didn't feel anything either.

Elgorn smiled.

'Just as I thought,' he said. 'The potion is strong enough to make one fall in love and strengthen a feeble feeling of affection, but it is useless if the person is already deeply in love.'

'We will never know if the potion works or not, will we?' she asked him.

Elgorn bowed his head, conceding defeat.

'Leave us,' she told him. 'I'd like to talk to Tristan alone. And if you even say one word about us to anyone else, I'll have your tongue roasted on coals and then fed back to you.'

Elgorn smiled unconcernedly and left them.

'So, what are we going to do?' Tristan asked her.

'I have no idea,' she said. 'I was hoping you'd have a way out of this.'

There was no way out and they both knew it. She could not abandon the ship with Tristan and run to the woods to start a new life. It was pure fantasy to believe that such a thing was even possible. She would have to marry King Mark when they reached Cornwall.

'I'll devise a plan to stay close to you,' Tristan said. 'I know that you can't reject King Mark and I'm not asking you to do that. I believe in our love, enough to trust that it wouldn't fade away so quickly. In time, we will get used to being together yet apart. It is the only way we can remain close while also fulfilling our duties.'

Isolde wanted to speak, but for the first time in her life, she had no words to express what she was feeling.

Why had God made her fall in love with someone with whom she had no future? It was cruel and unfair. How she wished she was a common girl, someone who didn't have to carry the weight of so many expectations.

The sun was setting. Isolde had begun her journey to Cornwall with thoughts of dying and now she had found someone with whom she wanted to spend her life with without any hope of worldly pleasures.

There were tears in her eyes as she kissed Tristan. For one moment, she wanted to be completely unafraid and open about her love for him. And when he took her in his arms and embraced her, Isolde surrendered without protest.

At that moment in time, all the people on the ship were magically distracted from looking at the two lovers locked in embrace. Elgorn, sitting in his usual place, smiled warmly at the lovers and went back to sleep.

Vladimir Lenin and Inessa Armand

Inessa Armand closed the door behind her and walked down the steps to the garden in front of her house. It was chilly outside, but she had a shawl that she now wrapped around her as she took a turn around the garden. As usual, she was thinking about Lenin.

They'd been quarrelling through letters recently and the topic was love or, freedom for women to choose whom to love. Unsurprisingly, Lenin dismissed her views by reminding her of the bourgeois origins of freedom of love and how society was likely to be sucked into a despairing abyss of debauchery if this was allowed. It didn't matter how much she tried to explain, Lenin did not want to understand that love could be elastic and freewheeling. In this aspect, he was entirely rigid and unwilling to

---

This story comes from Russia.

learn. Inessa had grown frustrated and hadn't been able to reply to him. She was unable to understand how he, of all people, could be so blind to the power of love.

Inessa turned around sharply, feeling overwhelmed. She felt entirely helpless. It was important for her that women didn't just get equal rights as citizens of Russia, she also wanted to release them from the bonds of emotional and psychological cuffs that men had tied around them since the beginning of time. Lenin, however, thought otherwise. To him, freedom to love was something only bourgeois women could afford (it wasn't, Inessa thought) and he was interested in the topic because it presumably clashed with his own ideas about the subject. (He didn't have any to begin with!)

It was all very tiring and time-consuming and hardly fruitful. Inessa knew that she would only lose by debating with Lenin about this further but she wouldn't back down because then she'd be handing him the satisfaction of an easy win.

She looked back at the house. Its long, narrow windows were slightly dusty, and the paint on the walls had chipped at many places. The ivy that lingered on the gabled roofs had dried and hung limply over the edges. The house had a forlorn, haunted appearance. It looked unoccupied because there had been no attempts at repair for years. Inessa couldn't find the time and she didn't trust anyone else with the job.

She sighed, grabbed her gown and started again. The house, ugly and despairing as it was, held a special place in her heart because of the days she had spent in it, talking to Lenin.

They used to talk in the study because it was her favourite place in the entire house. The candlelight reflected from the mahogany shelves and the sleek spines of the books stacked close to each other. There was a large table in the centre of the room with two chairs at opposite ends. Vladimir always sat at the head of the table with his elbows on the table, his chin resting on his clasped hands as he listened to her talk. He had suggested that she should drag the chair closer to him, but Inessa reasoned that she would be his equal in this position. Sitting beside him meant being closer and yielding to his presence. Lenin laughed and shook his head.

He seldom smiled in public. She found it odd. You could still be a revolutionary and have a sense of humour, but he had to uphold the image he had created in people's minds, and she could hardly blame him for playing the part so perfectly.

She did not want a perfect life. That sort of thing was an illusion. A falsehood perpetuated by people who thought happiness could be tied up in a bow and served to women without offering them any choice. She knew there was no real solution to the problems that plagued Russian society. The wounds of inequality and subjugation had festered for too long for them to be fixed by a band-aid. Or maybe the only way to bring any definitive change was to let the old world die and wait for the birth of a new one, start afresh. Inessa didn't know how long that would take but knew it would arrive too far in the future, after she was gone.

It had been rather easy to fall in love with Lenin. He was a man of consummate intelligence and respected it in return. Yes, he was rather plain and had a wry temperament, but then again she had never gone after beauty anyway. Chiselled faces bored her, and syrupy declarations of love made her laugh. She liked the papery stillness of a face wrinkled with age. She desired the touch of someone who had toiled with his hands in the late hours of night. She wanted to talk until the melted wax slipped off the table and dripped down to the floor. There was no complete way to love someone because every man and woman could only give a little of themselves to their loved ones There could never be utter submission. Of course, she had heard about the martyrs and sages who spent their lives dedicated to one celestial being without having encountered him or her in real life. Inessa believed it was because they were mentally ill. There was simply no other reason that a person should spend a life obsessed with someone whose existence can't be ascertained by any scientific means. People love what they could see, touch and feel. The demented, the unruly and the tragic built monuments to immortalise their love while others who were more practical minded knew to keep it separate from their lives lest they also slip into the mire of everlasting love.

Inessa wanted her freedom to be absolute. She would never depend on any man to make her happy. It was too grave a responsibility to bestow anyone with, least of all men, who had no idea what to do with themselves most of the time.

What about Lenin then? Was he different from other men? Did being ideologically and politically apart from other Russian men make him all that different from how he had been made to see women as creatures who were naturally weaker and beneath the male species?

Lenin would emphatically deny all accusations of prejudice and discrimination. And it was true that he believed in equality. He listened to the women around him with great interest and took their advice. He wanted to make Russia a great country, stripped of all the vulgar interests it had accumulated over the past centuries and remake it with the idea of equality between classes and sexes. It was easier said than done, though, because old habits don't die so quickly and dissent could build up anytime. The easiest thing men learnt in any corner of the world was to hate women.

Inessa sighed. She drew the shawl closer to her body. The evening had taken on a purplish hue and the trees that lined the villa had acquired a silver sheen that made her feel like she was a lost woman in an alien land. Nature seemed to have absorbed all the noises from the surrounding places, and even the crickets and little insects that wouldn't stop chirping on other days had quieted down.

Inessa let her shawl trail behind, graze over the short grass as she walked, and let her thoughts unravel.

She thought about her children. They were growing with the impression of a woman who flickered in and out of their lives without ever remaining fixed so they could form a proper image of her in their mind. It couldn't be helped. People mistook women's ambition for a betrayal of their maternal instincts as if it was something that every mother shared. Inessa loved her children, but they were separate from her ambitions.

And where was Lenin in all this?

If her mind was a hive of ideas and people with their narrow cabinets, Lenin occupied a space bigger than everyone else. Inessa did wonder if she was not wrong in admiring Lenin in a way that went against all she stood for. Outwardly, she wanted women to be free of men's influence, but she had tethered herself to a man. It was a vicious conundrum and she had given up any hope of ever resolving this knot of complication.

Inessa turned to look at the faint orange rays of the sun peep through the skeletal tree branches and had to hold herself lest she fell into a daze. The view had transformed into a still painting. The rising glow of the evening drowned in the watery haze of the dying sunlight. The air was fresh and clean and undisturbed by noise. It was a miraculous sight and Inessa wanted to absorb it into her soul so that she'd never forget it.

She knelt on the grass, turned and lay down on her back.

How many women had gone mad in love with men they couldn't have, she thought as she stared at the darkening sky. Some men died for women and killed for their love. Their stories were plentiful and filled the libraries around the world. One could get his hands stained deep red with the blood that these men poured out of their broken bodies and split skins just in the pursuit of what was unattainable. Women scarcely ever featured in the retelling of such stories and unleashed passions. They were almost always behind the fluttering curtains, their tender palms clutching a tear-streaked handkerchief, looking out through the grainy fabric into the distance, waiting for their beloved to return. Men who devoted their lives to love became heroes, and women who did the same became martyrs. Martyrdom was meant to be pure, and clean. It couldn't be selfish, or reckless like heroism. It seemed that even in the matters of love, one way or another, women were always losing.

Her mind was unsettled tonight. It just wouldn't remain on one thought. She didn't know whom to blame for it, but it seemed like she had come to the end of something that she couldn't quite identify and so couldn't move on either. She was in a state of self-induced stasis. Not going anywhere, just circling, being pushed by forces she couldn't control. She wondered if this was what madness felt like. Just a series of repetitions, like a strip of film, stuck in her mind.

And just so, her mind went back to him and the beginning of their relationship.

Inessa had always loved Lenin's eyes and their deep, weathered gaze. She tried to catch him in moments when nobody was looking at him and when he was free for just a few seconds so she could almost get a grasp of the man in solitude. He had once told her that he felt alone all the time. It was a typical thing for a man of his stature to say and she had felt an intense desire to counter him with a withering remark. But she had restrained herself because she had seen his eyes scan back to a private place of existence where even she couldn't reach him.

'You only ever exist between the moments, not inside or outside of them,' he had told her when she'd asked about his flights of absences.

He was less cryptic in his letters and if she was honest, that was how she loved to communicate with him. Face to face, she felt that something was lost between them. As if he was afraid that he'd reveal something of himself that he did not mean for her to see. In his letters, however, Lenin was frank, wise and rigorous. He was thorough in his arguments and never shied away from criticising her or receiving feedback that could help him untangle his thoughts. In her role of a confidante and friend, Inessa had achieved a perfect combination of interests that a lover can achieve. It was exhilarating.

Nadezhda, Lenin's wife, had turned out to be surprisingly benevolent toward Inessa even after she'd found out about her husband's interest in her. She'd embraced Inessa wholeheartedly. At first, Inessa had been surprised and a little cautious. They had barely known each other at the beginning of her affair with Lenin. It had always been clear to everyone who met them that Nadezhda had a mind of her own. Nobody could ridicule her or call her a secondary foil to Lenin.

'People are afraid of new experiences,' Nadezhda said when they had met a few weeks earlier. 'They're so keen on maintaining the perfect image of normalcy that they forget to try anything that would disturb it.'

'Am I a distraction then?' Inessa asked playfully. 'Am I someone who storms into one's life to pull him from beneath his bedcovers before passing into oblivion?'

'No, no,' Nadezhda said. 'I didn't mean to offend you. I see you as a force of nature that gives life, not a storm that uproots and destroys it.'

Nadezhda placed her hand on Inessa's wrist.

'It is easier to love someone from a distance than being near them' Nadezhda said, her brilliant eyes shining with kindness. 'Lenin is never going to wholly belong to either one of us so I don't see any problem in sharing him with someone who might love him as much as I do.'

It could've easily been an empty thing to say. And for a moment, Inessa did feel that Nadezhda had given her permission (if such a thing was even required since Inessa had little patience for the bourgeois definition of love that had seeped into the minds of even the staunchest of communists) less out of her own volition than as a sense of defeat in the face of her husband's decision to stray, but looking into her eyes she saw the blaze of genuine care that couldn't be faked by simpering smiles.

The wife stepped out of her way. It was so crass and ridiculous. This sentimental self-assurance that one could drudge up from her swollen core to satisfy their lust and unrepentant desires. Of course, the only way to love someone was to submit to them wholly. The martyrs and maniacs, the goddesses and whores – all of them were bound by their desire to be wanted by other people. Love was ravenous and spiteful and sometimes tender. People went about in circles, delirious when struck with it and then fell to the side, exhausted and incomplete.

Inessa sat up and clasped her arms around her knees. A thick strand of hair fell across her eyes, blotting out the view before her but she wasn't looking to see anymore. She was thinking about her recent meeting with Lenin.

They were in Paris. Lenin had come to help her read the riot act to KZO. He was staying with the Mazanovs and she had gone to visit him. The evening sun had waned by the time she stepped into the hall and saw him sitting in the corner. He was leaning against the wall and his eyes were closed as he listened to the music.

Inessa went and sat near him, but she didn't disturb him. She looked at his face. She lingered over the pencil-thin lines around his eyes and mouth. Lenin wasn't handsome but his face had the hard impression that suggested a face that existed outside of time and was untethered to the ideas of conventional beauty.

A shadow passed over his face, and Lenin blinked his way to consciousness.

'How long have you been watching me?' he asked her, pushing his coat down and shuffling up to sit properly.

'Not long enough to see you slip into a trance,' Inessa replied.

Lenin smiled. 'I didn't know when it happened. I had started to dream even before I shut my eyes.'

'What did you see?' she asked him.

'Colours,' Lenin said, and his eyes widened in wonderment. 'A cascade of them, like a parched stream filling with the blood of the sky.'

One of the most impressive of Lenin's talents was that he could paint entire worlds by his careful selection of words. He could turn a straightforward sentence into a poetic reprieve, or a slashing assault if he wanted to. And it never took him any time to think, which was what surprised her the most because she knew the strain it took to make language truly sing and pulsate with vitality. He could do it without wrinkling his forehead. Inessa decided she was more envious of him than in awe of his gift.

'I'm exhausted,' she said.

Inessa hadn't expected to blurt out the truth so easily but the bounds holding her back had loosened and she hadn't been able to stop the words from tumbling out of her mouth.

Silently, Lenin stared at her face for a moment, as if trying to discern something that wasn't apparent.

Then, in an action that shocked her as much as it warmed her heart, Lenin took Inessa's hand in his and pressed it softly. He didn't say a word because there was no need. They spent the moment in total silence, looking, reading each other's face rather than expressing whatever emotions that were flitting between them.

background, someone began to play the piano The sultry female voice carried an air of pathos. g was about two parted lovers who meet each er years of separation. It was a very maudlin and native song, Inessa remembered later, but in that om, with the peach-coloured lighting of the bulbs ed the walls faintly caressing their skin, it served lm to their worried thoughts.

Inessa started. She had fallen asleep on the ground. It was night. The sky was as black as spilled ink. Clouds covered the crescent moon, drenching every corner of the villa in darkness. She sat up, and took a long, deep breath. Suddenly, she felt a lot lighter. Her mind had become unburdened and she knew that even if Lenin didn't accept her prospectus about love in writing, she would show him that freedom to love was just as sacred as being bound by it.

She stood up, the shreds of grass falling away from her gown, and went inside. She had to write back to Lenin.

Amrita Pritam and Sahir Ludhianvi

They stood on the balcony. Sahir was smoking and staring at the purplish clouds in the distance as the evening sun dissolved in a sedate manner. The flat overlooked a busy street and it had been overflowing with people since the morning. It was Sunday, after all. Amrita had glanced down to see a crowd accumulated around a man and his dancing monkey. The man's singing was dry and ragged as if he had dangled a razor down his throat and scratched the tissues until one could trace the blood in his voice. Amrita turned away and leaned against the balcony wall.

'I keep thinking about white pigeons in mid-flight, shot down by a little boy who loves to torment animals,' she said.

This story comes from India.

Sahir, staring ahead, didn't turn to look at her. He parted his thin mouth and softly blew a jet of smoke.

'Well, gruesome images make for excellent poetry,' he said. 'Violence is easier to describe than love. It is also more versatile.'

Amrita knew that he didn't really believe this to be true, but he was in the mood for a discussion and nothing was easier than urging her into a state of combat. He'd let her counter and destroy his reasoning. She'd smirk knowingly and he'd shake his head. Amrita had got to know this trick a while back, and played along when she liked it. It was important for her to keep a balance in their relationship. She didn't want to give him a sense of ownership in this game, that he was the one to decide when to play it.

Today, she was in the right mood, and the topic was interesting enough that she was sure he would share his genuine feelings about it.

'It's not,' she said. 'Anyone who believes that violence endures longer than love shouldn't be responsible for any kind of art.'

It was a sharp, direct jab and it landed directly where she had intended. And she had intended it to wound. It was up to Sahir to take the bait now. He smiled, but not in the way that signalled a quick response. It was vague and less certain and for a moment, Amrita thought that her words had struck him deeper than she'd hoped. However, a moment later, his expression cleared and this time his smile reached his eyes.

'Love is eternal, indeed,' he said, tapping his wrist on the top of the wall to flick the ashes. 'I'm glad that you corrected me. And isn't most violence just a response to frayed bonds of love? It is also the end-point of obsession, which itself is love taken to extremes.'

Whenever he talked like this, Amrita noticed a glow that emanated from his pockmarked face. It was a glow that didn't just make him more beautiful, because it had to do with something other than beauty, it made him seem less obscure. He seemed to possess the rare quality that rendered everything he wrote to be comprehensible even in its complexity while he wrapped himself in layers of mystery. He didn't do it intentionally, Amrita realised, it was just the way he was. He could only truly be himself in his writings and even though she got to know that it was the reason he could never truly submit to his emotions, she had begun to notice the stirrings of this distance between them.

Amrita would've liked him to caress her hair, rake his fingers through the tangles and resolve them. She would've liked to hold his hand and feel the warmth of his skin against hers. She would've liked to fall asleep with her head on his shoulder while they watched the monsoon drizzle from the narrow window of her flat.

She wrote his name on any surface that she touched. Her fingers would scrawl his name across walls, and metal canteen tables, rusted rails along the stairs, on tree barks and silk fabrics. By printing his name everywhere, she could feel his phantom presence beside her.

Sahir was reticent, which made her cautious. She

didn't want to do anything that'd make him pull away from her. They never discussed what was between them directly. It always came up in their poetry, or in their conversations. Amrita had confessed her love for him in her poems, but Sahir hadn't reacted enthusiastically or even acknowledged it. Sometimes it occurred to her that maybe they had unknowingly entered a contract of silence over their relationship and could only ever talk about it in passing. What was more frustrating? Thwarted desire or self-denial?

She remembered their time in Lahore, when they'd met at *mushairas* where Sahir used to read his poems. He was always serene but firm in his recitation. He believed that the urgency of his poetry was enough to move the audience so there was no need for behavioural embellishments.

Amrita, sitting among the poets who looked at her with a mixture of nervousness and suspicion, gazed at him with growing interest and awe. She followed the texture of his voice, the way it dipped slightly when he wanted to stress a word to signify its importance. She was attracted to his unassuming manner and his indecorous way of social critiques in his poems. And yet, none of his writings were lathered in self-pity or apologetic beseeching. They were slashed with terse and wounding rhymes that made people take another look at the grotesque and unequal world they had created. In this way, they were beautiful. Like a bouquet of roses with sharp blades jutting out of their stems instead of thorns.

One evening, she approached him at the end of the

mushaira. Sahir was reasonably shocked that she'd chosen to talk to him instead of the perfumed elite around her.

'I've always wondered if angry art actually achieves its intended goal or if it only works to push people away from looking clearly at their own sins,' she said, smiling.

Sahir looked down, then up, preparing a response for her. She was quick and merciless, and he had to keep up with her or she would lose interest in him.

'People will always refuse to accept their wrongs,' he said. 'But they will always appreciate beauty.'

Amrita laughed and gestured with her hand that they should walk together to the exit.

They walked in silence, uncertain of what to do. Amrita wanted to say that she admired his courage to write about tough subjects with brazen, stripped-down lyricism while Sahir wanted to confess that few had the gift of turning the most heart-breaking images into transcendent poetry.

They didn't talk about anything of the sort. They didn't talk at all. Somehow, as they walked side by side, words ceased to matter. It wasn't because they couldn't get themselves to say anything, but that their shadows leaning against each other and the fact that they were present in that moment alone, without the intrusion of the outside world, carried more meaning than any words ever could.

There were many other occasions where they spent whole evenings just looking at each other and contemplating the feelings between them. Sahir's career was steadily taking off while Amrita continued to dazzle the literary world with her talent. It would've been so simple. They could've got married soon after they met but it wasn't possible. Amrita didn't know why she had never been able to love her husband, Pritam.

She had tried her best to understand him, but she'd realised that the only reason she couldn't connect with him on a deeper level was because he didn't possess any of the complexities that attracted her to a person. He was very simple and unambitious. He was satisfied with his life and cared for his wife and children. He and Amrita didn't have anything in common and thus not even their silences were expressive and alive with unspeakable feelings. She didn't believe that Pritam was intellectually unevolved. The problem was that their temperaments didn't match at all, and she knew that living a compromised life was just as bad as living a lie. She was aware that leaving Pritam would mean casting a stain on her reputation and there was no certainty that Sahir would be able to accept her and her children.

All these doubts remained at the back of her head, but she could never bring herself to express them out aloud. It was also possible that Sahir himself knew of the hurdles in their path. He couldn't not know, but chose to remain silent because he was counting on her to broach the subject. And even though she knew that sooner or later she would have to set her desires aside and think of everyone else and make a decision, Amrita still couldn't do it. She just wanted to spend a few moments with Sahir before everything fell apart.

In the meantime, she continued to meet Sahir and let herself be swept up in the gale of love.

'In any lovers' lifetime, there are few moments when they are truly in love,' Sahir had told her once. 'In those moments, they're not only together physically but mentally as well because they are not only practicing it but also thinking about love.'

Amrita thought about it for a moment. She had never felt anything of the sort with Pritam, but she had experienced something similar with Sahir many a time when they had met even though they had remained silent the entire time.

'I believe you,' she said. 'The idea of loving someone sometimes supersedes the need to be close to them.'

Sahir's face didn't betray his emotion, but he kept looking at her as he took one last drag on his cigarette and blew a feeble cloud of smoke. He flicked the stub away and excused himself.

Amrita picked up the stub and put it in her purse. She'd started collecting his cigarette stubs that she smoked in his absence so she could feel the warmth of his breath on her own. A few days ago, she had scribbled his name across her notebook in a state of romantic fugue. She had folded the papers and then put them in a locket she had bought. It was evidence of her worship, her love, which was her only religion.

She had stopped praying to God a long time ago after the death of her mother but she had never let go of her belief in the divine. Divinity, for her, was not the promise of a divine being that hid in the upper layers of space. It was the connections she made with people. Her children, the nature, and spending time with Sahir that made her believe the force of love was stronger than any scripture could preach. She would cherish these fragments and consider herself touched by God, because in the end, didn't the almighty's word, in any language and culture, turn to the incandescent nature of love of every kind?

Amrita placed her hand on the warm spot where Sahir had been sitting and closed her eyes. These little acts of momentary submission to the amorphous residue of Sahir's physical form were the closest they would ever be. Everyone knew how to eroticise the mundane and the unattainable. You could cut away the parts you didn't want and keep the ones that were less likely to hurt. Amrita collected these transient feelings as souvenirs, abstract impressions made up of creased shirts. Like stroking the lip of a red rose, she could have a taste of Sahir's physical beauty only in the interstitial moments of their meetings.

Time passed. The country was split in two and the separating lines were jagged and there was bleeding on both sides. The bodies dribbled out of packed train compartments, cracking their chins on the dirty ground, with gaping mouths, dried blood streaking their hair. She'd seen people's feet with deep, scarlet scratches from running barefoot over dust-coated platforms. She had seen the bodies being dragged by their torn clothes. What struck her later was the ruthless impartiality of death. The way it could strip an entire life off the body so that in the end it wasn't anything but a commingled mass of flesh and bones. There was no time to sit down and think. The violence had left lesions across the bodies of two countries that would never heal.

Amrita and Pritam decided to move to New Delhi, India. Everything happened so fast. Amrita felt as if she was among the millions who were sleepwalking through the streets of their new home because they were yet to fully absorb the cataclysm.

And where was Sahir all this while? She had let the idea of him slip past her mind and into its velvet depths. He did float up to the surface a few times and when he did it felt like a jolt of electricity ran through her arm. She still wrote his name on every surface that her fingers could find, it was a habit that had become a ritual ingrained in her soul.

She heard when he went to Bombay and started writing for the film industry. She was happy for him. He'd finally found a way to convey his hard-hitting messages to people with the help of the most infectious form of art. She'd often listen to the songs written by him in the evenings during moments of solitude and try to imagine if he could've still written so well if they had been together. Very likely not, as she had realised that separation and thwarted desire fuelled artists to make great art than any muse or relationship.

Her last meeting with Sahir, or the one after she found out that he'd fallen in love with someone happened in her flat in Delhi, after which nothing was the same again.

Pritam was gone by then, and she had made a home of the things she cherished most in life. She was in a good phase of her writing career and had finally managed to settle into the arrhythmic pace of the city.

'How did you find out?' Sahir asked her, setting the cup on the table.

'I read it in the newspaper,' she replied.

They were silent for a moment.

'I wish it was different,' Sahir said.

Amrita didn't understand. What exactly did he think should have been different for them to end up with each other? She wouldn't want to be any different than she was and she wanted the same for Sahir as well. There was no point in trying to remake the past in one's mind.

'I don't,' she said. 'I'd rather have our moments to myself. You're free now from the guilt of ever having loved me.'

The words felt like a sharp stab in Sahir's heart and he winced.

'I never felt guilty for loving you,' he said. 'I only regret that I wasn't able to meet you before all this.'

'I hope that you keep her happy,' Amrita said, cutting him off.

Suddenly, she wanted him to leave. She couldn't face him anymore. There was nothing left between them. It was over.

'I'm sorry,' Sahir said, his voice flecked with pain,

'You're not sorry,' she choked. 'I know you're not.'

Sahir stretched out his hand, in the hope that she'd

take it. But Amrita kept sitting where she was. He let his hand fall and stood up.

'I'll go then.'

'Wait!' Amrita said before she could stop herself. 'I can't… I can't be happy for you. I can't accept that you won't belong to me anymore in any shape or form.'

'That's not true at all,' Sahir protested, even though he knew that they had finally come to an end of their undefinable love story.

'I had given up hope so I can't say that I was completely surprised when I got to know about you and Sudha. I just find it strange that you could fall so easily in love with someone else. What about our love, what about me? I was wrong. Deluded. You are free to love anyone you want, and I should respect your decision and yet all I feel is hatred toward you. And this hate will consume me until there is nothing left so now you have to tell me how I should go on.'

It was pathetic how far one was willing to degrade oneself for love. And loving someone was as degrading as it was liberating. Amrita had known this for a long time and she had wanted to avoid any embarrassment that would result from confronting Sahir directly, but she couldn't help herself. It had to be done so she could move on. To strip herself bare before she could pick up the pieces to remake her heart. To release the demons of resentment before she could let the sunlight in.

Sahir sat down next to her. He tried to take her hand in his but didn't, couldn't.

'I waited for so long. Was I stupid to believe that you'd ever be brave enough to accept me? Yes, I was.'

All those words she had written for him. His name on the fabric of earth.

'I will never say that you fooled me or lied to me. You never responded in any way that could have ascertained your love for me, but I knew it was there. It was there and then it wasn't. I had my doubts when I thought that all women love in the same way while the men do it differently and not with the same intensity or honour and I was right.'

She spoke a lot and with a lot of venom. Sahir listened to her and didn't say a word. When she was done, Amrita felt lighter, as if all the poison had been drained from her body. She felt liberated.

'And yet, I can't see you being destroyed by guilt and powerlessness,' she said. 'So, I release you from the duty of loving me. If I can, I will try to move on from my misery and try to find someone who can love me without the fear of the unknown and the unfathomable.'

'I hope you find him,' Sahir said. 'You will find him.'

What a stupid thing to say, Amrita thought. He was trying to handle her with care, as if she'd break if he said something harsh.

It was time to say goodbye. Amrita followed him downstairs and watched him until he disappeared in the crowds. She went up, took out her notebook and pen and started to write.

***

Sahir felt a dull pain just beneath his ribcage as if someone had violently pulled out a chunk of his flesh. He walked the Delhi streets aimlessly. The meeting with Amrita had not gone well. She had reached a tipping point, and then fallen into a rage-filled daze of operatic emotion that he had seldom seen. He understood her perfectly well.

In a way, he had betrayed her. But the only reason why he had never revealed his emotions to her was because they had been unknown to him. He never thought as clearly, as bravely as Amrita did and perhaps that was his failing. If he had been able to articulate what he felt, like he did in his writings, to her, maybe their story would have been different.

What he was left with now was certainly not meagre memories. They were precious, luminous moments that were etched with the blade of destiny in his soul.

He'd remember her later, but only in flashes of images that ran swiftly across his mind, as if a reel of film passed through the projector so fast that nothing was legible on screen. If he lingered over any one moment that they had spent together, Sahir was afraid that he'd spend an eternity staring back at it and punishing himself for letting her go. Amrita was the smoke he had accumulated in the cavities of his organs, she had done irreparable damage to his body while giving incomparable pleasure to his soul.

Amrita-Sahir. Sahir-Amrita. Amrita. Sahir. Complete in their incompleteness. Alone and always together. In the end, all lovers become stories that people tell each other in augmented versions. These stories become histories that travel forth and then back to the moment it all began.

Back, back, back till they recede to faint outlines of themselves, fainter than voices from a broken-down radio, fainter than light caught on a pane of glass in winter, so that what remains are not stark images of letters folded in shirt pockets and wavering smiles but memories of those moments, like words erased carelessly but still visible to anyone who would look long enough to read their story from the beginning.

Adele Hugo

I wish my father would stop asking me to come back. He has been persistent, unyielding in his pleas. All the letters he'd sent had been dripping with his strained kindness that I know would've hurt his soul to put down on paper. At first, he only made benign requests. He wished I was with him to look after mother. Then, after he realised that my resolve had hardened even more and I had passed the Canadian border to meet *him*, his interest in my whereabouts transformed into an agitated, wounded beseeching. The kind that makes daughters weep quietly into their handkerchiefs and return to their safe homes with their heads hanging in shame. I wasn't like those women. I had a higher purpose that I was destined to

---

This story comes from France.

fulfil. My father's drooping spirit could not send me back home. I had reached a place beyond his influence, vast as it was, could not enclose my heart anymore.

He still believes that I escaped because of the murmurs of my unsettled mind. The whispers that led me astray and made me follow a twisted path to my doom. He doesn't understand. He never will. A woman's love is more mysterious and deeper than a man can fathom. I have chosen to walk away from the shelter of my family to pursue the wild, flaying miseries of the real world. I have disturbed the pool. The water has mixed with dirt and will never be pure again. My father keeps calling me back as I travel further and further away from him.

But this is not a story about my father. He has already filled tomes with his stories. This is the story of my love with...

At first, I didn't find him special. He was handsome but had a smirking, preening presence that had repulsed me. It would be ungenerous to call him obsessed with his own self, but I prefer to be truthful than kind. With his dark, wind-blown hair, deep-set eyes the colour of winter sky, high cheekbones, slender nose and petalled, bowed lips, he could've been a subject for a Renoir painting. He was a soldier stationed in my city. As a member of the troops, he used to march past our house and look at me standing on the balcony. I don't know why I continued to stand there even after understanding that he was up to no good. He'd stare at me shamelessly, expecting me to stare back. He walked with his back straight and stamped his feet on the paved ground. I was wary of him. The way he'd rake his fingers through his hair and smirk; yes he smirked, somehow it felt wrong to call it smiling because the light never reached his eyes. He was made in a way to resist a way into his mind. He could never be happy, only amused. I should've been warned that his gaze was clinical and spare. It fixed on a person and pulled them apart as if probing what was the most valuable thing that throbbed inside them. He wasn't concerned with feelings. He wanted to annex the body and then fling it somewhere he wouldn't have to see or feel pity toward them. His world was clouded where even the shadows had sharp, jagged ends that ripped to shreds whoever was foolish enough to pass them.

I was young and troubled. My father's reputation rested like a brick on my throat. I could scarcely breathe when I saw people whisper his name with the kind of reverence only reserved for the divine. He was a genius and an artistic colossus. I shrank back from him. The whispers were dipped in honey, but they tasted sour to me. I was afraid that he'd die one day, and the people would turn against us. They'd rip my hair out and call me a bourgeoise whore who had swallowed their food while they begged for morsels in the streets. They'd slit open my stomach and stuff their hands inside until they found my organs and wrenched them out. I imagined their faces sticky with my blood as they gobbled my entrails.

To calm myself, I used to sit in my room and write for hours. I wrote about my daily routine and what I had for breakfast and lunch. I wrote about how green the trees surrounding our house looked in the morning. But then, come evening, they'd turn black as tar and their drooping leaves resembled the wings of bats hanging from the arthritic fingers of the dead that had risen after the last rays of sun had retreated from the face of the earth. Unlike my father, I had no great themes to write about. Like every frivolous young girl, I wrote about wanting to love and be loved. To be loved, you first have to create a mystery around yourself, which is easy if you're a mysterious person but very difficult if you, like me, have no sense of self. How could anyone be curious about me if I had no idea what was curious about me? A lot of the girls I knew had more knowledge about men that I didn't. They'd tell me about their conquests and I'd stand beside them with my mouth slightly parted like an imbecile who couldn't even understand the meaning of simple words. Their eyes would widen as they gesticulated wildly about having exchanged letters with a boy or a quick peck under the shade of the trees or under the stairs of their very homes while the household chatted upstairs. I felt dizzy with all the information they gave me. It was too much but a lot of it was useless for me. I didn't want any of the things they wanted. I just longed to disappear and wanted nobody to remember me.

That should have been a warning. The moment one begins to harbour rebellious feelings is when nature decides to turn its fury against them. I wanted to be alone because I had always been lonely. And because I had never been able to form a connection with anyone. I was baffled that he showed so much interest in me.

I still remember the day I met and talked to him. Summer was in full bloom and I had been invited to a ball by one of the esteemed families in the city. It was a lush affair. The ladies twirled in the hall, their heavy gowns arcing gracefully as they danced with their partners. I was sitting in the corner and twisting a strand of ribbon around my fingers when a shadow fell over me. I looked up and saw him smiling down at me.

'May I?' he asked, nodding at the place beside me.

'No!' I said curtly and looked away.

He bowed his head and moved away from my sight but didn't leave.

I busied myself with the ribbon but felt his presence, imposing in his silence.

'What do you want?' I snapped, dropping the ribbon on my lap. 'I have seen you looking at me from the street. I know you don't come with good intentions, but I'd still like to know them before I can call the police and ask them to put a leash on you.'

I saw a brief flash of anger pass over his face like a streak of lightening illuminating the sky for a moment before disappearing into the darkness.

He smiled, bowed his knees a little and stretched out a hand toward me.

'I'd like to dance with you,' he said.

He was baffling. I had just insulted him and warned about taking severe action for his audacity to approach me. And yet he showed no sign of stepping down from his decision to court me.

'And why should I give you the honour of dancing with me?' I asked him.

'I'm the best dancer here among all the men who are struggling to draw their feet to the rhythm of the music,' he said. 'I will only compliment your beauty and elegance. If you say yes, that is.'

I agreed because I wanted to get rid of him. He looked pleased with himself when I held his hand and let him steer me to the dance floor.

He hadn't lied. He was a good dancer. Precise and fluid, without the hesitancy and clumsiness of the men around us. He looked directly at me. There was a challenge in his eyes. He had electric blue eyes. I could stare at them for hours and still not find any solution to the mysteries swirling in them.

'I hope you're pleased,' he whispered as he swirled me around.

'You appear too concerned with what pleases me,' I told him. 'And that's enough. I'd like to take a rest now.'

He held my waist firmly and took me to a corner, away from the prying eyes of the crowd.

'You're beautiful,' he said. He was leaning too close to me with one hand against the wall. I stared at his throat and the taut skin around his Adam's apple. I had a sudden urge to kiss him and had to look away.

He leaned closer. I wanted to trace my fingers over his lips. I wanted to devour him.

'Will you marry me?'

'What?' I said, thrown back into the moment and startled anew.

'Will you marry me, Adele?' he repeated.

His smile grew hazy. His lips melted into a blur. I flinched and stumbled back into the wall.

What did he mean? He wanted to marry me? How was that even possible? We barely knew each other and I had made my dislike for him very clear from the beginning. Did he take me for a fool? How easy was it to influence a timid woman into falling in love with yourself? Did I look stupid enough to agree to marry a stranger?

'No, no, no!' I had meant the words to come out in a stream of scalding fury, but I sounded scared, almost distracted.

He looked confused and started to say something, but I pushed him back and ran away. I didn't wait to hear from my friends and left in a hurry.

I didn't come out of my room for three days. His proposal had sent my soul into a state of stupefaction. I retreated into myself and shut down my thoughts until all I was thinking about was him and those five words. How brazenly he had said it! Did they even mean anything to him and if they did, was I really capable of that kind of long-lasting affection? I didn't consider myself unlovable, but the speed and conviction with which he had uttered the sentence had plunged me into prolonged introspection about myself as a girl on the cusp of unfurling into a woman.

My father would protest and throw tantrums, but he'd agree if I simpered long enough. He didn't seem to come from money, which would make my father happy. To see his stunted, dithering daughter being reduced to rags in a stuffy flat would satiate his desire to see one of his children suffer exactly the way other people did. He'd deem it a good education.

As much as I wanted to defy my father, I also had to think about the practicalities of marrying a penniless soldier. That I was even contemplating saying yes to him meant that I had already yielded to him. I had given it a lot of thought and found that despite my reservations about him, most of which I had imagined, there wasn't much I held against him. I had focused on his abstract nature for too long to give any thought to his emotional form. What was under that pristine and slick beauty? The splintered mind of an unfeeling man or a placid reserve of feelings that was waiting to be discovered by someone? I could be that someone. I could pull out a newer, purer man out from the depths of his hard shell. Life would be easier with him as well. I could be a different woman, freed from the shackles of responsibilities of being Victor Hugo's daughter. Here was a way out of the strictures of my life into something uncertain, brave, and happier. I threw my bedcover on the floor, pulled open the door to my room and nudged the windows open to let in the sunshine. My father pretended to worry about my health, but I put his concerns to rest with an airy remark.

'I was meditating,' I said. 'I'm completely fine and I'd like to go outside for a walk. Alone!'

Once outside, I walked straight to the army's station

and enquired about him. He was at home. I went straight to his flat and greeted him with a bright smile when he opened the door.

'I accept your offer of marriage,' I told him.

I walked inside and turned to look at him. He was dressed in night clothes and his hair was tousled. He scowled at me, an expression that surprised me, and then went to wash his face. When he came back, he was ready with his reply.

'I don't want to marry you anymore,' he said.

I started, as if he had slapped me twice in quick succession.

'What do you mean?' I said. 'When you asked me to marry you, I was confused and didn't know if you actually meant it. I didn't say no to you, it just came out in a moment of disruption. I'm not confused anymore. I will marry you.'

'Didn't you listen,' he snapped. 'I don't want to marry you now. I'm not interested any longer. Go away.'

'But how can that be? You were ready just a few days ago and now you're not. What made you change your mind? If you think that I was unnecessarily rude, I apologise for my behaviour. Let's not linger over past arguments. I will tell you when you can approach my father with the formal proposal and when he accepts it, we can marry later this year.'

He shook his head as if I were a child who was asking for candy when his pockets were empty. I didn't understand why he was so angry. His displeasure didn't have any hint of mirth that would have lit his eyes to show that he was lying and making fun of me for coming after so long a time. Later, we'd both laugh at this tense moment when it seemed that he almost hated me for everything I'd done.

He sighed, his shoulders sagging as if he was suddenly very tired.

'Adele, listen to me. I don't love you and I don't want to marry you. Yes, I had proposed to you that day and maybe we would've got married if you had agreed but after you declined, I realised that you weren't really that special and my affection toward you had just been a mild infatuation that was doused after you exit the scene. I feel nothing for you. I never did.'

'That can't be true,' I whispered, more to myself than him.

'I think you should leave now, Adele,' he said and when I didn't stir from my spot, he firmly caught me by the elbow and pushed me out his door.

'You'll find a good husband, Adele,' he said, looking at me with his cold eyes. 'Your father is, after all, a great man. I doubt if he would let his wayward daughter go into the hands of somebody lesser.'

He closed the door on my face. I stood there for a long time. Longer than I can even begin to count but I only know that it was deep into the night when I reached home and my room. I went to sleep thinking about scary things that seemed too real sometimes but they always had an end.

I started writing letters to him. I told him that I understood that he was intimidated by my father's reputation. I didn't care about my father. I wanted to be with him and if it meant waiting till he was comfortable with his earnings, I was ready to wait.

His replies were tepid and unsatisfactory, but I found reason and hope in them. I knew he loved me. He'd just slipped into a moment of crisis because of his feelings of inferiority of birth and uncertainty at his place in the world. Meanwhile, I started to prepare for the time when we'd be married. I looked for a better place to live and new clothes. I found a publisher who was interested in printing my writings. That could support us for a while and I was sure that he'd put even more effort into building our family.

I was ready for everything, but we had to be careful, so we restricted our meetings. He was still on duty most of the days and I couldn't get out of the house at night, so we continued to talk through correspondence.

For a while, I really believed that we were settling into a sense of desired normalcy until he was called upon to serve in Halifax, Canada. He had no means to pay for my travel and I couldn't stay in France while he had to work. I decided to take the money that I had saved and followed him across the seas to another part of the world.

I have not been able to talk to him properly since I arrived here. The one time I caught his attention he tried to act like he didn't know me, perhaps because he was with an officer and didn't want to reveal my identity to him. He is so thoughtful.

I am living in a boarding house run by a kind couple. I intend to stay there until he can get time off from his duties and we can get married. There is nothing more humiliating than asking my father for more money, but I can do it if I can persuade him to give his blessings to our union. He will purse up his lips and give curt replies but, in the end, he will be happy for me.

I have waited for years to be with him and with the passing time I've had the sense that I am in an entirely different plane of existence, in contrast to everyone around me. For them, love is an ordinary way of life. Something that they must contend with. It's a duty for a lot of them and for some it's a crime, a release of inhibitions. But to me, it's worship and my altar is dedicated to that most amorphous entity. Love.

I wait for him to come back to me. I spend my time thinking about him and writing about love. I have made it my mission in life to spread the message of love because there is nothing more sacred than love. I will continue as long as I have to, until people hear me. He hears me. I devoted myself, body and soul to him and nobody, not even he, can take it away from him. When the body perishes and memories fade, nothing remains but the spots of love staining the earth we once walked on. To be destroyed by love is a blessing not everyone gets, and if that is my fate I must accept it and fulfil my destiny.

Simone De Beauvoir and Jean Paul Sartre

She'd met him in college. They were in the same class, and both were extremely competitive. Simone knew that she had to work twice as hard to achieve her goals because nothing was easy for women. She wanted to compete with the best because she had high standards. There was no joy in defeating mediocre men in academics. They didn't care enough to be humiliated, and since they would always be preferred to women, they didn't lose anything, even when someone like her came first in the class.

Sartre, however, was different from the very beginning. And not because he was particularly good-looking. Skew-eyed, bespectacled, and short, he could've

---

This story comes from France.

easily gone unnoticed in a crowd. Physically, he had not much to recommend him, and later she'd run to others to satiate her carnal needs. But he was also one of those who have a fullness of experience while still young. And that was what drew her to him. He was not radiant. He did not have the presence that filled one with the hope that something good awaited them. In all honesty, she would realise later that he had more casual contempt for people than anyone she'd ever met. And yet, she was enamoured by him from the moment they started talking.

Paris was a disgruntled city in those years. Its beauty had been marred by the pretentious bourgeois idea of beauty. It had been cheapened and trussed up to resemble the water-colour pictures of postcards. A fantasy as imagined by the idle ruling class which only knew how to hoard things until their gullets were full.

Sartre shared her contempt for the apathetic and gluttonous bourgeois which made their interactions easier and far more fruitful than conversations with others on the campus.

He wasn't an easy person to be with, but Simone never believed that he'd be the only man she'd have a relationship with, which made a lot of his eccentricities easier to accept. And he had some qualities that were so unique that she continued to love him even after years of being with multiple lovers. She didn't like to think of love as something that belonged to only one person. That was selfish and harmful. Love, if not shared with others, could turn obsessive and destructive. People were afraid to accept that they were inherently incapable of creating a single lasting relationship. That was why most marriages, even those based on true love as they thought, were so unsuccessful. Once they realised that all the mysteries had been answered and there was nothing left to know about the person, love came to an end. With Sartre, she seemed to be on the cusp of discovering new things about herself and the world around her every day. Only he could provide her that escape, the guarantee of sane knowledge.

They'd meet daily in cafes and talk about every topic. Many times, their conversations rambled from one topic to the other and they lost track of time. It became a habit. It wasn't necessary that their discussions reach any meaningful end. There was no hurry when debating over a topic. They would let it hang around them like smoke from their cigarettes and wait for it to settle. As she had made clear in the beginning of their relationship, they were both equal.

And what about feelings? For Sartre, feelings were just an extension of intellectual stimulation. He didn't think a person could have genuine feelings if he or she didn't have intelligent thought. Simone was opposed to the idea that human beings were worthy of having emotions only if they put them to good use. Everyone had his or her own capacity to use their minds. They shouldn't be discriminated against based on their intellect. She found it difficult to connect with Sartre on numerous topics. And maybe this was the reason why they remained together for so long. He could always be relied on to hear her arguments and then present his own. Between them, they found a middle ground that worked. Simone knew that his ideas were just as radical as hers and wouldn't find acceptance in society easily, but she was ready to fight them with reason and her own explanations.

Paris, being a hub of activity, was buzzing with people and ideas in those days. As ugly and depleted as it had been allowed to become, she could still find a way to enjoy its ample attractions. She knew that she had to make a life independent from Sartre. He was only a part of it, but though significant, he wasn't indispensable. She was free to choose any one she wanted to spend her time with, and she did exactly that when she was annoyed with him. He was stubborn and so was she. They had decided to give each other the time needed to decompress before continuing their affair.

Meanwhile, she was free to discover what she liked and disliked. The world was too vast to be stuck on one thing and it was always better to go out and experiment.

Simone was surprised when she realised that she liked women as much as she liked men. To her, the feeling of attraction had never been alien, and she had never denied it. What had been more difficult was to find someone belonging to her sex who reciprocated her feelings. She knew the dangers of revealing one's true identity to the public. It wouldn't take long for them to tear apart what they felt was an aberration. It was all nonsense and Simone looked forward to flouting such restrictions soon, but she had to be discreet for her own safety as well as the other vulnerable party.

She'd met Emily by chance but they had recognised each other in one swift moment of eye contact. Emily worked at a pastry shop and smelt of cinnamon. She was in her early twenties, with strawberry blonde hair and big eyes. Her dress sense was immaculate and she spoke with such confidence that people were fooled the into thinking that she knew everything there was to know about a particular subject.

Simone wasn't looking to engage with someone who would pour their intellectual musings on the platter every time they met. There was a time and place for everything and as much as she liked to spend time with Sartre, he couldn't help but be severely analytical in ways that tended to be enervating if she stayed with him for too long.

So, she'd taken up with Emily to quell her boredom and to fulfil her need to have some fun. She had been careful before she approached Emily for a coffee. And Emily had been reluctant. But instead of being scared, she was curious. But she couldn't meet Simone because she had to be at home to take care of her ailing mother.

At first, Simone wondered if Emily was one of those sentimental and exasperating women who lived for their families and forgot that they had an existence separate from their duties. But Emily surprised her on their first date altogether. For one, she despised her family for shoving all their responsibilities on her while they lived off her salary, treating her like a servant. The only reason she hadn't left was because she didn't have any money and couldn't afford a place to live.

'But I'm saving,' she told Simone. 'And I don't know when, but there will come a time when I will be free of them and then I'll decide what to do with my life.'

'That's wonderful! I wish more women would get out of their homes and make something of themselves even though such a task is difficult in a society that deeply hates women,' Simone said.

'Of course, it does,' Emily replied. 'It hates everyone who appears weak. People love to pick apart other people because it's fun to see someone ruined.'

Simone was relieved that Emily wasn't just another self-deprecating woman with no sense of humour and plenty of words to waste on their misery. At times, Simone was astonished by her ability to be so unsparing when she described others. She had erected a tower in her mind, and while perched on it, she judged everyone because then it was easier to choose the ones who were worthy of her attention. She knew this kind of behaviour was absolutely unnecessary and alienating and she had stopped trying to make excuses for people a long ago. Most of them didn't care about each other anyway, and even less for someone just passing through their lives. Even if she made severe mental notes, which she kept to herself, there was no harm in the practice.

She told Sartre about Simone and he was amused at first but then happy for her.

'Good for you,' he said. 'Have fun!'

'That's it?' she asked him. 'You're not jealous or upset?'

'Why would I be?' Sartre replied. 'It's your life and you can do whatever you want. I can't stop you from making decisions relating to your lovers.'

'Right,' she said.

Simone was touched, but also frustrated by Sartre's laidback attitude toward their relationship. A small part of her had wanted Sartre to throw a tantrum or at least show some emotion that would assure her that he had warm feelings for her. Romantic jealousy, it seemed, was not one of the emotions that Sartre had ever felt, which explained his detached, scholarly manner and ability to see things from a distance to better derive meaning from them. Simone couldn't understand why she even cared for his reaction, since his ability to stay neutral was something she had cherished in herself as well. And yet, here she was, pursing up her lips as Sartre went back to his reading.

Later, she would wonder if it was this exact moment that led her to mistreat her lovers in the future. She wasn't sure about the point of inception, but it definitely did contribute to her unjust behaviour toward them. But when she looked deeper within herself, it was a bit of Sartre but a lot of her. She couldn't have been as cruel to Emily if she hadn't had that streak in her to begin with.

'What do you mean?' Emily asked. 'You're bored with me? How? We have only known each other for a few weeks. I thought you were happy!'

Simone tapped her wrist on the edge of the coffee cup she was holding, letting the cigarette ash fall on the floor.

'Yes, I was. But now I'm bored. You have been very

good, but I don't think I can stand much of your whining anymore. It was wonderful while it lasted but let's not prolong each other's suffering. You can leave.'

'Bitch!' Emily screeched. 'You think I'm your servant. You act like I was here only for your enjoyment and now that you're full, you don't need me anymore, eh? Is that what they teach you at your big university? To be as inelegantly cruel to someone who loves you as possible!'

'You're upset right now, but I know you'll understand how this is the best outcome of our relationship,' Simone said. 'You are a very beautiful woman who has the talent to bake the finest cakes. But you're emotionally undeveloped and naive. If you were a bit older, not in age but in experience, I could see us dragging this relationship for a few more months, but since your youth is the reason for our lack of connection these past days, I'm afraid there's nothing you can do about it.'

Emily screamed and cursed but Simone remained unmoved by her tears. She let her unburden herself but told her curtly to leave once the hysterics were over. Then, she immediately called Sartre and told him she wanted to meet.

Sartre listened to her tale intently and she made sure to make it as juicy as possible. It had become clear to her that he was one of those people who was aroused by stories of romantic disasters. She told him everything, every little detail. She sculpted her words around Emily's ruin with such perfection that he was hanging on to every word, his book lying face down on the table.

It was better than sex and they both knew it. Stories were, after all, the most effective way of seduction and Sartre was finally able to submit himself to her after listening to the way she had emotionally flayed an innocent woman. It was cruel and awful, but it was the only way he could open himself to her. It was perfect. They continued like that through their lives and found the perfect balance of love and professionalism that few have experienced.

They were alike in ways that two people seldom are and they didn't put each other on the marital pedestal so there was no fear of unravelling. Simone was astonished that she had found such harmony relatively early in life and that her relationship with Sartre never lost its vigour. She was fortunate because what the two of them had been able to achieve was so rare and precious that the fact that it was never destroyed by their own wilful natures was almost miraculous. Maybe it was because of their mutual interests, and understanding, but as much as she would've loved to put character traits as a reason for their success, the truth was much simpler – in its own, dry, despicable, individualistic and charmless way, it was love.

Johnny Cash and June Carter

Music brought them together and made them recognise each other's soulw as similarly crafted by the almighty. She was like a song. Yes, that's how he'd describe her if he could. She was a feeling, a transient moment in the morning when the sun shone at its mildest and transmitted warmth and a sense of hopefulness to shrivelled-up beings on earth. He could've spent an eternity just looking at her, forgetting to move from his spot and still consider his life satisfying. Of course, it wasn't so easy. It was never easy. Professionally, he was at the top of the game. He was glad that people connected to his music and that he was able to give them something to hold on to albeit briefly.

This story comes from America.

'I feel like I know you already,' she'd said, her eyes sparkling, when he'd told her that he had always wanted to meet her.

They were backstage, standing in the narrow lobby that led to the dressing rooms. Johnny turned and looked at the slender gap left by the half-open door and into the silver glare of the bulbs that lined the mirrors.

'What are you staring at?' June asked him. She craned her head in the direction of the make-up rooms and then looked back at him. Her face was still but it wasn't without feeling. Actually, it occurred to him that June was among those blessed people who were able to express a multitude of emotions with a flicker of their eyelids.

Johnny wished he was similarly talented because he believed that he felt things too intensely and in a way that he couldn't articulate. He wanted to unknot the sadness that had clotted his heart since his brother's death. In a way, he believed that singing had become a way of exorcising the grief that had seared itself into his soul.

'Sometimes I just drift, and keep drifting,' he told her. 'I like disappearing into moments when nothing is happening.'

June smiled. 'That's such a beautiful way to put it,' she said.

Johnny looked at her, and she looked back at him. And in that moment, it was clear to Johnny that he'd love this woman forever. He knew it could be a joke. He could be mistaking momentary desire for a deeper attachment, but he had never felt the sudden surge of overwhelming love for any woman.

And with this realisation came the mounting anxiety that June was married. He realised that he had just got himself into something he had no idea how to get out of. He didn't know how to deal with this feeling he had developed for her except to keep it buried inside him. It shouldn't spill out in an unguarded moment of desperation or he risked alienating June and disrespecting her.

'I'd just… just a moment.' He fumbled and shuffled to the exit before June could stop him.

Out on the street, he bent down and clasped his knees. He was shivering. This weakness, this sense that he would lose control if he was in the presence of a particular person was so unique to him that he suddenly felt reborn. That he had not been awake for a long time and now he was untethered by the cord that had restrained him and finally free.

June decided to accompany him on his tours. Johnny was surprised when he heard that she'd like to sing in his shows. In his mind, he had ruined their first meeting. June was charmed by him and didn't consider him strange at all. She still looked at him as if she were trying to sort out a puzzle.

'I don't have any secrets,' he told her once when she asked him what he was thinking.

'I know, but you have secret feelings,' June said. 'And they can be more dangerous if they aren't let out of the mind.'

'What if my feelings aren't as complex as you think

they are?' he said. 'They might just be pretty little nothings that go nowhere and do nothing.'

'No feeling does nothing,' June said. 'You can't describe some feelings because they are too complicated even though they might only seem complicated. Easiest things are the most difficult to describe.'

'Your sentences are like whirlpools,' he said. 'I can't ever find purchase on them before I sink down to the bottom.'

June shook her head and laughed.

'My sentences are just as simple as I am,' she said. 'Maybe you're special to find deeper meaning in them.'

There was something mischievous and secret in June's smile. At the same time, when she smiled, Johnny felt that he could stand taller in the world, fearless of its uncertainties. She was the person with whom he felt safe. Their world was hardly without people. It was filled with incredible sounds and swirls of colour and it could be overwhelming for him sometimes. He didn't know what to do with himself if he wasn't writing or singing.

And what about Vivian?

Johnny was embarrassed to realise how little space his wife occupied in his mind. Once, she had been the love of his life, and he still cared for her. But something had changed since the day they first met and fell in love. It wasn't that he had become bored or that Vivian had become less interesting. He had always been in awe of her strength and the way she could stand up to people without inviting their derision. She was caring but she didn't treat him like he was any different. People and fans might treat him differently, and fawn over him, but she never deteriorated into a simpering wife. Vivian was as she was. She lived without illusions and that was her greatest quality.

All this was good, and in his lowest moments, Johnny castigated himself for even thinking about how he'd begun to see that maybe he was not meant to be with Vivian after all. Every morning when he woke up beside her in bed, he felt more removed from her. He had hoped to spend his entire life with her but now it seemed impossible. He blamed himself. His own inability to be free of himself, get out of his own head, was the reason for his failing marriage.

He didn't have the strength to say all this to Vivian so he tried to ignore his feelings and hoped that they'd go away one day and he'd be able to love her again.

What he couldn't even hope to do was to think of stop loving June.

He couldn't reckon with either of these discoveries, so he took the easiest way out by submerging himself in the soothing anaesthesia of drugs and alcohol. In the silvery daze of amphetamines and barbiturates, he didn't have to look past himself. He could just drift into the foggy depths of sedation and forget that he had to make any decision that concerned his life.

He would be gone for days, unaware of anything happening around him. He was numb to any feeling, and he was grateful. It was better to feel nothing than to feel too many things that could destroy your life. Days later, when he emerged from the fugue, he'd look at reality like many cracks in a mirror so that every complication was multiplied and made grotesque. He had to be awake to make music. Sometimes he wondered if anybody would care about him if he were to stop writing and performing songs. There were no guarantees in showbiz, and it was very likely that he'd be abandoned to his fate. People went in the direction of the noise; they didn't like to be in the company of silence. Stillness, after all, was just another word for being dead. He wanted to die but he was too cowardly to do it. Maybe if he continued to inject poison into his blood, one day that would do the job for him.

'Let's go for a drink,' June told him as they walked away from the stage.

Johnny felt that his face would just melt into the sweat. He blinked away drops of perspiration and glugged a whole bottle of water. He leaned against the wall and looked up. He waited for his breath to return to its normal pace. The floor seemed to move beneath his feet. His head was filled with noise.

'Yes, yes, let's go,' he stammered.

They went to a small bar just down the street. June, who didn't have a hair out of place even after their rigorous session on the stage, ordered two martinis.

She then turned to look at him and said, 'It'll be alright.'

Johnny didn't know if it would, but in that moment, he believed her.

'It gets tiring after a while,' he said. 'Sometimes, I

wonder if there is any point to all this. People hardly care about the meaning of the lyrics if they can jive with the tune and have a good time.'

'And is that such a bad thing?' June asked. 'If people are jiving and having a good time, it means that your song has given them precious moments to distract themselves from their lives. You're giving them moments they'll remember late in life and smile about. That's wonderful.'

'Not just me, you too,' he said. 'I wish I could be as open on stage as you are.'

'But you are. You give all of you on that stage and that's more than anyone could ever say about themselves.'

Johnny wanted to feel relief, but he was too restless. The dim lights of the bar pricked his eyes and he was still sweating profusely. He didn't want to make a fool of himself in front of June. She couldn't know how messed up he was because then she'd look at him with pity in her eyes and that was something Johnny didn't need.

His hands shook as June handed him the drink and he had to keep blinking to keep his vision clear.

'So, what do you do in your free time?' he asked June abruptly and a little too loudly.

'Well, I hardly get any free time,' June sighed. 'With the kids and everything at home…'

She let the sentence hang between them. They had never talked about their personal lives and their mutual silence had felt like an agreement to never broach the subject.

'It's the same for me,' Johnny said. 'I mean, in a different way, it's the same.'

What was he doing? He couldn't even form a sentence without tripping over himself and making an absolute joke of himself.

'I understand what you mean,' June said. 'It isn't easy to write a song with the whole house making a racket in the background. But I find that sometimes the best ideas come out of the chaos around you.'

'I don't know. Chaos scares me,' he admitted. 'I get the feeling that I might just get lost in it if I'm not careful.'

'You're too obsessed with getting lost and being alone,' June said. 'I assure you, people aren't as scary as they appear to be. You just have to learn to trust them.'

'I know, and I do trust them,' he said. 'But it gets overwhelming after a while. I need to separate myself or else I tend to turn petty and aggressive.'

June put her glass down on the counter and grabbed his hands. She led him to the centre of the hall where a few couples were dancing and put her arms around his shoulders.

'You need to relax,' she told him.

The lights that had seemed to poke at his eyes had suddenly turned mellow and soothing. June's touch was warm and his skin tingled beneath her touch. Johnny let her lead. June threw her head back, and laughed as they glided across the floor to the tune of Ella Fitzgerald.

With June, he could still hold onto a part of himself that hadn't been ravished by drugs. He could submit to her and let her take him to places where they sat and talked and contemplated life. Surrounded by the thrum of music and the battering mundaneness of his domestic life, he had only a few moments to himself and he spent them entirely with June. They had no name for their relationship. They were more than friends but not lovers. They hadn't confessed their love for each other but there was no need to do so. It was very clear that they loved each other. But it wasn't so easy. Johnny was responsible for Vivian and his kids and June had her own family to deal with. They couldn't walk away from people who loved and cared about them. It was worse than cheating, it was a betrayal.

Vivia had sensed that he was acting even more indifferently than usual and wanted to talk about it.

'I just don't understand what I'm doing wrong,' she said to him. 'You are always distant. Always in your own world. I can never reach you. And then with all the drugs and…..'-

'It's nothing,' Johnny said sharply, then lowered his voice. 'I'm sorry. I wish I understood myself better so I could tell you more about what I'm feeling. But I don't, so I can't. I assure you that it's not your fault at all. I'm the one who isn't up to it anymore.'

'What do you mean?' Vivian said slowly. 'You're not up to being a husband and a father?'

'No….. I mean, yes,' he said. 'I mean, no. I don't know.'

Vivian's expression soured. 'Can you, for once, be sure of anything in your life?' she asked. 'I'm not going to sit here and see you go back and forth, deciding if our marriage has ended or not. I need you to answer me so I can also move on. I know you don't know a lot of things but at least have the decency to tell me the truth.'

'I don't know.'

'Yes, you do,' Vivian said. She was trembling with barely contained rage. 'Just tell me the truth. I know you don't love me anymore. You haven't been in love with me for a long time. You and I both know that. The only reason you haven't decided to leave is because of the children. But I'm not as weak as you think I am. Just tell me the truth and set me free.'

And he did so.

Vivian was surprisingly calm during their discussion. She listened to his stories of adultery, that she'd always suspected and his uncontrollable addiction to drugs. She made good points that his lifestyle was unsuitable for their daughters and that they should remain with her till they grew up. Johnny agreed to her demands.

The divorce plunged him deeper into the velvety depths of depression. He couldn't go a day without drugs. His life had shattered. He didn't have anyone to support him. Everyone had disappeared suddenly, as he had expected. He was alone.

June came to meet him on the third day of his breakdown. He saw her standing outside his house. She was wearing a simple grey dress and a hat. He hadn't bathed in days. His eyes were bloodshot, his hair tousled, and he was in his pajamas. He went to the door, opened it and welcomed her inside.

'Hi!' June said, but he turned and shuffled inside, unwilling to let him see her.

Johnny walked into the kitchen, turned on the stove, turned it off, turned around and looked at June standing before him.

She took his hand into hers.

'Let's sit and talk,' she said.

She led him into the living room and seated him on the sofa.

'I know what happened,' she said. 'I'm sorry. But you can't let it destroy you. You have a life to live.'

'Do I?' Johnny asked hoarsely. 'It's better if I die. It'd be easier for people to remember me in death than talk about me while I live like I'm the worst man in the world.'

'That's not true. Don't believe what the trashy media has been writing about you. They write to sell more copies, not to tell the truth. I know you are not the worst man in the world. You may not be perfect, but then again, nobody is.'

Johnny sighed and sank back into the cushions.

'I don't know how to live,' he said.

'Well, nobody does. And yet, we do it,' June said.

They were silent for a moment. Then, abruptly, June sat up and looked at him.

'I'm divorcing my husband, she said.

Johnny was dumbstruck. He sat up as well and turned toward her.

'Why?'

'Oh, you don't know?' she asked, a hint of sarcasm creeping in her voice, 'I love you. I have loved you for a long time. And now that you are single, I want to make sure nobody swoops in to claim you this time. I want to spend my entire life with you. If you want to, of course.'

Johnny stared at her for a long moment. Then, he started to laugh and then he started to cry.

He couldn't believe himself. It was a miracle. He had never let himself believe that June would feel the same way about him. And here she was, confWessing her love for him with such frankness that he was surprised and grateful. As June took his face in her hands and brushed away his tears, he swore to himself to get better. He had to get better for her. He had to get better because he had to start living his life again. And this time, with his eternal love by his side.

The Girl and the Superstar

Let's begin with the cliches. It is easier to talk about things people know, or think they know. To dispel any illusion, you have to acknowledge its existence. It's real, and it's not.

You could say the same thing about me as well? At least the way you've looked at me for years.

The striking eye-liner, the teetering bouffant, the lacy shirts and flowing dresses. These things are very real. They are easily identifiable and couldn't be mistaken as belonging to anyone else. They've made me who I am.

But they're an illusion, created to hold a girl upright in front of the slashing flashlights of cameras. To make her seem someone she's not so that the people watching

---

This story comes from America.

her wouldn't get confused as to how she got hold of this superstar. To make her extraordinary, and turn her into an idea and an image. To distil her, until she's not there anymore to hurt anyone with her ordinariness.

I first met him at a party thrown by him.

I was young, and didn't know how to act in front of confident people. I'd been invited to the party by one of his friends, but he was nowhere to be seen when I arrived. Nervous, dressed in a plain peach sweater and a wool skirt, I watched as men and women around me mingled and laughed, drunk on alcohol and the good spirit of the evening.

I declined an offer for a drink, and went to sit in an empty chair. Parties are no fun when you're surrounded by strangers, and have no idea how you should behave. Watching everyone in a jolly mood made me feel jealous and useless. I'd decided to leave quietly and undetected, until he arrived in the room and everyone turned to look at him.

I'd only seen him in pictures, and once on tv. I was obsessed with his songs. I'd cut-out his photos from magazines and pasted them in my scrapbook. I was already in love with him before he even knew who I was.

I sat upright, crossed my legs and folded my arms over them. He was talking to one of his friends. The man mouthed my name. He nodded slowly, and turned his head to look at me.

I froze. Something tugged at my heart, a string tied to my ribs unravelled. I felt exposed under his smiling gaze. He'd directed everybody's attention to me, and with it, their curiosity.

I smiled, and got up from my chair as he came to introduce himself.

'I know, I've heard you on the radio.' I said, after he told me his name. It was supposed to be a joke, but he didn't laugh.

'I see,' he said, 'So, are you enjoying yourself?'

'Yes, very much. Everyone is so lovely.' I said.

It was one of several lies I'd tell to keep him happy. What shocks me now is how easy it was to lie, how liberating to just agree with whatever he said without thinking of anything because he always believed me. Or pretended to believe me.

We talked some more. He told me about his band, and how sad he was about his grandmother's death. He confessed to finding parties too loud and abrasive. He liked to spend time alone with his friends but it was so difficult because he was so famous.

'I understand,' I said, 'I also feel that way sometimes. When I'm at school and everyone's making noise, I just want to leave and sit with my thoughts alone.'

He smiled, 'I guess we're similar that way. Alone, even when we are with people.'

It was one of the happiest days of my life. He was so different from what I'd imagined himself to be. Famous people were supposed to be haughty and cruel, always looking down at you from their high perches, judging you for not being special like them.

But he was different. He cared deeply about what I thought, as I realised after I met him again, and he treated me like he'd treat any other adult. Not as a child.

At school, I had to talk with silly girls and mannerless boys. It was very stifling to sit in a room filled with boring, unintelligent kids and being taught things by obnoxious teachers who thought they knew everything.

My parents were concerned with my meetings with him.

'She's still a child. It's a lot.' I heard my mother say this to my father once.

He'd invited me to another party, and even visited our home to take permission from my father. My mother just couldn't understand why he was so interested in me. She thought I was just a new flavour he was trying, before he got bored and discarded me.

'He's world-famous. He keeps a different company. She's too young to be meeting older men.' She said.

My father was a stern, patient man. He knew how dangerous men could be.

'He came here and promised to keep her safe.' He said, 'I think we should trust him. He seems to like her a lot.'

'But you don't understand'-

'I understand all of your fears.' he said, 'I'm scared for her too. But she wants this. She has promised to complete school before they do…anything. I trust her to not blindly give in to her urges. She'll be fine.'

***

I was in love with him.

It felt like love. It couldn't be anything else. He made me feel special, and loved. When he looked at me, I could feel the warmth of the entire world taking me in an embrace. I loved his voice. I loved his eyes, and his hands. I loved the way his throat worked when he sang. I loved his eyebrows and the way he looked at me from across the room. I loved his touch. I loved him, I loved him, I loved him.

'You should try more make-up.' He said.

'What?'

We were in his car, on our way back from a party. I was wearing a dress he'd gifted me. It was pale blue, with sequins and it brought out the colour in my eyes.

'Yes. I want you to look better than every woman in the room.' He said.

I was suddenly self-conscious, and touched my face instinctively to check if I didn't have a pimple or a boil spoiling my look.

'Don't you like how I look?' I asked him. 'I don't do a lot of make-up because it makes me look too old.'

'But that's good.' He said, and put his arm around my shoulder, 'You'll look better in a more mature makeup. You're almost an adult, now, aren't you? Well, won't you agree that it's time to start acting like one?'

I hesitated. I'd seen the women in his circle. They were all stylish and pretty. They had a strong sense of confidence that I couldn't hope to mimic. I always felt insubstantial beside them, which is why I spent all my time at parties by his side.

I wanted to look older, yes, but I didn't want to copy someone else and feel bad about myself.

'You're right.' I said, 'I need to look better when I'm with you. I need to improve my sense of style so you won't get embarrassed in front of your friends. I should not be selfish.'

'Good, very, good,' He said, patting my head, 'I will set up a meeting with the best stylists in the city.'

'Stylists?' I said, a little alarmed.

'Yes, baby, I can't trust you with anyone else except professionals.'

He was so kind, so considerate. I couldn't imagine any man who'd go to such lengths to care for his girlfriend. I almost teared up, but instead of crying like a little girl, I kissed him deeply. A tiny gift for all he'd given me.

***

I won't lie, his world was disorienting. He was a superstar, after all. He had a manager, and a group of friends who were always by his side. His family lived in a big mansion, the kind of gilded architecture that could swallow a person whole.

He left me there when he went on tours.

I moved in with him after I realised that there was no point to my existence if it couldn't be shared with him. My mother shed tears. My father turned to stone. I left my old self without any regret and apology.

It wasn't an easy transition to his vaunted lifestyle.

His popularity was at its raging peak, which meant he had to spend a lot of time on tour. I couldn't accompany him on tour because it was too hectic.

So, I spent my days wandering the cavernous halls of his mansion and tried to get used to the way people lived there.

I tried, I really tried, but without his presence, everything felt colourless, depthless and empty.

There was no scarcity of luxury at the mansion, but there were rules to abide by. I couldn't go outside because of his fans crowding the gate every day, or stay in the garden for too long because cameramen hounded the vicinity, looking for a juicy picture to set the news aflame.

With nothing to do, I spent my days turning pages of storybooks or lying sprawled on my bed.

When he came back from tour, it was like the sunlight had pierced the confines of a dark cloud.

He took me in his arms when I ran up to him. His smile was enough for me to know that everything would be fine.

'Please don't go away again.' I whispered in his collar as I wept, 'I can't live here alone. It's too lonely. I'll go mad. Take me with you next time. I promise I won't create any trouble. Please, please, keep me with you always. Always.'

He laughed, lifted me up, and said, 'Yes, always. Always…'

***

It had been a few years since our marriage. We were having dinner. It was late at night, and there was no one else in the house. I'd told the help to retire once they served food.

He had been in a volatile mood lately, flying into a rage over the slightest provocation. His music was doing fine, and he was still loved, though, not as much as he used to be. Perhaps, it was the decline in public favour that stung him. I'd seen him poring over magazines in his room, staring at the big headlines that heralded the era of new talent. He was scared that people would forget him and move on to someone they thought was sexier. I could feel the jealousy radiating out of him, souring his looks. His words turned terse and ugly, laced with a bitterness that comes with the realisation that even the most revered can be replaced without warning. The drugs had started to chisel at his beauty. They'd leached the light out of his eyes. He was hollowed out. The image of him that I had wanted to preserve in my mind was finally splintering. Once it cracked, and the pieces fell away, there would be no putting them back into place.

'Do you think I'm a good man?' He asked.

I knew I should say yes. It was the easiest way to placate him, to ward off his insecurities. He wanted assurance and I was there to provide it to him. It was the only duty that had remained unchanged over the years of our relationship. I was supposed to say yes, because any other response would be too honest and cruel.

Am I capable of cruelty? I thought. Can I tell him

that he's worthless now? That all the glitter is now rotting on the ground. The glamour is gone, smeared on a rumpled shirt hanging in the closet. The fans are gone, howling for another pretty face gyrating his ass on stage. The sycophants are gone, whispering their poison to some other victim. Only I remain, still standing by his side. Pretending that everything is alright, and that he's safe in the warmth of my embrace. He's nowhere to go now. I'm his anchor, holding him in place.

'No, I don't think so.' I said.

He blinked, and put his fork and spoon aside.

'Why not?' He asked.

I folded my napkin and placed it back on the table. I had lost my appetite.

'You've always been selfish.' I told him, 'You've always put yourself over others. Your family, your friends, me. The only thing you've genuinely loved your whole life is music. It made you what you are today. What could you have achieved if you were simply good? Goodness is a virtue for people who don't have anything else. They like to brag about their goodness because they have nothing to show for their years on earth. Goodness gets you nowhere. But you had talent and you were smart. You made use of what you had to build an empire. That takes a lot of hard work. I'm not saying that good people aren't successful, but you don't get to the place you are by playing nice with everyone.'

He was silent for a long moment. I waited for him to smash his plate on the floor or wrench the tablecloth and throw it aside. But he remained still, pinned back by my words. I couldn't read his expressions, the storm brewing behind the placid facade. He could be angry, and not show it. He was very good at being deceptive with his moods when he wanted to take me by surprise.

'Did you ever love me?' He asked.

I suppressed an urge to laugh. I couldn't get away from that question. All through the years we'd been together, he'd lobbed this query at me like a neglected child who wanted constant assurance that he wasn't alone in the world. In the beginning, it felt innocent. A minor insecurity that could be assuaged with a simpering smile and a wet kiss. Over time, however, I'd gotten the sense that he wanted me to say that I did not love him. The tone of the question, which had been honest and sheepish, had curdled into a mockery of my feelings toward him.

Do you love me? Did you ever love me? Are you capable of love?

I sighed. 'Yes, for a long time.' I said.

'And not anymore?' He asked.

'Things have changed, you've changed.' I said.

'And you can't love the person you see before you, now?'

'I don't think you want love.' I said, 'Love, for you, is an excuse to be worshipped.'

He frowned.

'Was it easier to do when we met? When I was richer, more popular?'

I laughed. Of course, he was going to bring in

money. He was still trying to hide behind the cover of his celebrity.

'I never wanted your money.' I said, 'You were the one who bought all those dresses for me because you thought I was cheap. You wrapped me in luxury because it was better for your image. You have always suffered delusions of persecution, you know. Everyone is always out to get you, even your friends and lover? That's why you run around seeking it. That's why all those women…'

I didn't finish the sentence. I didn't need to. He knew what he'd done. The women he'd gone to slake his thirst because I wasn't enough for him. I'd overlooked it because I believed that it was something these people were supposed to do. These artists with their wayward desires that were stranger than a girl from a little town could understand. I'd have been a fool to think that he'd always remain tied to me. While he prodded me for any evidence of straying, he fucked any woman who offered herself to him. We had never discussed his infidelity. It was a potentially explosive topic that could detonate our relationship and I had no idea what we'd do with the bloody residue in the aftermath. So, I'd stayed quiet and he'd continued with his philandering.

'I've always loved only you.' He said, 'The other stuff…it doesn't matter to me much.'

'Doesn't matter to you, yes.' I said, 'But what about me? What about my feelings? They don't matter to you either.'

'I've always cared for you. I've given you everything

you've ever wanted. Is that not enough?'

'No, not anymore.' I said.

'Are you going to leave me?'

This was my cue to lie and say no. Everything would be easier if I just lied. He'd go back to being nice, for a while at least, and I could forget things and tend to our children. It had always been so easy to just lie and go along with what he wanted, so why would it be any different now?

'Yes.' I said, 'It is the only way I can save myself, and you.'

***

I understand myself better now than I used to. I also believe that I only truly began to live my life after I'd left him. Once his shadow was gone, I was able to be my own self. I could finally realise things I liked and didn't like. I could wear whatever I want. I could make a fool of myself and not feel guilty.

His love had cost me the freedom of my soul. I'd been caged in his ideas and desires for such a long time that I cried happy tears when I realised I'd forgotten to apply makeup for the entire day.

It was the little things that I had to take possession over. To finally be able to see myself as me.

I did not stop loving him after our divorce. I didn't stop loving him when he died. I didn't stop loving him after people told me that what he'd done to me was wrong.

I think I'm still too naive, or just too much in love with him to accuse him of any crime. All I can do is be grateful to have loved once, and loved purely. Loved with abandon, with stupidity and clarity. Loved, in spite of all the glaring signs that told me to not. Loved, even when I was filled with rage. Loved, even when I felt alone in the entire world.

Because if I had not, I wouldn't have gotten lost in the darkness and made my way back to the light.